An East End Christmas

An East End Christmas

Elizabeth Waite

sphere

SPHERE

First published in Great Britain in 2015 by Sphere

A CIP catalogue record for this book is
available from the British Library.

ISBN 978-0-7515-6215-6

Typeset in Bembo by Palimpsest Book Production Limited, Falkirk, Stirlingshire
Printed and bound in Great Britain by Clays Ltd, St Ives plc

Papers used by Sphere are from well-managed forests
and other responsible sources.

MIX
Paper from
responsible sources
FSC® C104740

Sphere
An imprint of Little, Brown Book Group
Carmelite House
50 Victoria Embankment
London EC4Y 0DZ

An Hachette UK Company
www.hachette.co.uk

www.littlebrown.co.uk

An East End Christmas

Chapter 1

Carla Schofield was just eighteen years old, but the head she had on her shoulders would convince folk that she was much older. The harsh reality of life had long caused her to realise that money was an absolute necessity. From an early age she had always been able to laugh a lot, and that had encouraged people to laugh with her. She had grown into a tall, slim, confident girl with perfect clear skin and hair the colour of a polished horse chestnut. She was open and friendly and she loved every member of her family with no exceptions. Her mother Ellen had died some years ago.

'Stop staring out of the window, you do far too much day-dreaming.' Her uncle Sidney's words brought Carla up with a start.

'I've already mixed the porridge and put the kettle on,' she was quick to tell him.

She made the tea and held out a steaming mug to her uncle. 'Pass that to Grandad, will you, and put a couple of biscuits on a saucer for him. I'll get his breakfast soon.'

Grandad was such a dear, Carla thought. He had been only fifty years old when his wife had died, leaving him with four sons and a daughter. He had spent all his working life in the dockyards, and in turn, three of his sons had followed him there to become dockers – unskilled casual labourers. Only Fred, the eldest boy, had taken a different path. He hadn't liked the idea of being a docker and had started his working life as a telegram boy. He had proved his worth and today was a licensed waterman. Still employed by the Royal Mail, he had his own small craft which he used to deliver letters and packages to ships in dock.

Thousands of dockers, stevedores, lightermen, seamen and ancillary workers depended directly on the Port of London for a living. Any man who had a regular job as a docker was especially lucky. To get taken on as a casual labourer, there was a degrading system in force. Dozens of men, young and old, would be trying their best to get work. First they had to get past the foreman, an unpleasant man who enjoyed his power. He would have a handful of brass tickets, which he would throw on to the ground. The crowd of men would dive down, fighting and kicking in order to get their hands on one. The foreman thought it was the greatest joke in the world; sometimes he would even stamp on a hand that had managed to grab one of the tickets that would ensure a man a full day's work.

It was a hateful job, labouring in the vilest of weather on monotonous and often ill-paid jobs, without the slightest hope of better conditions. Yet to be made a permanent labourer at twenty-one was the height of good fortune. If a man remained on this grade until he was seventy, he was given the maximum pension of ten shillings a week.

Carla shuddered at her own thoughts. The times she had sat on the floor, resting her shoulders back against her grandad's knees and listening to him relate the terms and conditions of living within the dock–land area, and how families in the East End of London always came up smiling. She wasn't at all sure that last fact was entirely accurate.

All thoughts of the wrongs and rights of this life were suddenly driven from Carla's head by the clanging of tin cans being kicked along the road and the sound of running footsteps. Hastily she removed the pan of porridge from the gas and moved across the floor so that she could look out of the kitchen window. She knew what she was going to see, and it always made her smile. Six or seven young lads, all looking like ragamuffins, though there was no mistaking that they were full of the joys of spring, despite the fact that the morning was bitterly cold.

God alone knows how they got into the dockyards, Carla grinned to herself, but come hell or high water they managed it time and time again, and by the looks of it they'd done well for themselves today. Bits and pieces shoved under their jackets, pockets bulging, and their laughter ringing out loud and clear. Of course, they didn't get away with it all the time. When caught, their ears were practically pulled from their heads by the burly dock police, and for good measure a kick up the arse as they ran away. Still the local lads went back, especially when cargoes of fresh fruit were left lying about. The spoils they managed to shove up their jerseys always provided a little treat for them and their families.

Carla poured herself a cup of tea. She did not sit down to drink it, but began gathering her belongings together. As she did so, she thought what a wise old bird her grandad was. He still had all his marbles even if his limbs were not strong enough to enable him to get about as much as he would have liked. Smiling to herself, Carla remembered how much this elderly man loved to get involved in any political argument going. Last year Neville Chamberlain had returned from Germany waving a piece of paper which he'd said would guarantee 'peace for our time'. Grandad hadn't been the only one who hadn't had faith in that promise, and now it was generally accepted that the country was on the way to being involved in a second war.

It didn't bear thinking about.

Carla loved all four of her uncles and their wives and children, and was thankful that their marriages were happy ones. She also loved the fact that they all lived locally. But she couldn't help wondering where her father was now, and why he had gone away. No answers had ever been forthcoming. No quarrel had taken place, or so she had been told. When Grandma had died, it had seemed natural that Ellen, the only daughter, should stay at home and take care of her father. Then Leonard Kingston had appeared on the scene. He had moved into the house, and there had been talk of them getting married in the very near future. All in the garden had appeared to be fine. Then Ellen had become pregnant, and without so much as a goodbye note Leonard had upped and left. To this day, not a word from him and certainly no financial support.

As a youngster, Carla had often wished she had a dad, but that feeling never lasted long, and as she shook it off, she would always count her blessings. She was Carla Schofield. At school she was never punched, kicked or even teased. It was a well-known fact: you hurt one member of the Schofield family and the whole gang would be on you like a ton of bricks.

Carla finished getting ready and glanced in the mirror. 'I've laid your tray, Grandad, and later on Daisy is going to bring you a bowl of soup and a couple of sausage rolls. That should see you all right until I get home.'

'I'll be fine, gal. Stop yer fussing and get going.' Lowering his head, he peered up through the kitchen window at the rooftops. 'God almighty, there's been a heavy frost in the night. You mind how you go, pet.'

Carla bent over the old man, stroked his thinning hair and then kissed his forehead. 'I'll be fine, Grandad,' she assured him.

As she straightened up, she heard the street door open, and then the kitchen door was almost blown off its hinges by the force of the wind raging outside.

'Fred!' Carla screamed with delight, staring at her uncle. His cheeks were pinched and his nose quite red, but notwithstanding the cold, his mouth broke into a mischievous grin. 'What the hell are you doing here this time of the morning?'

In two strides he crossed the floor and flung his brawny arms around her shoulders. 'I got to thinking you might like a lift to work this morning, seeing as how it's cold enough to freeze the balls off a brass monkey. You can travel in a Royal Mail van just so long as yer keep yer head down.'

Carla smiled her delight. 'Must be my lucky day, eh, Grandad?'

'No more than you deserve, my pet. Must say, it does me old heart a power of good to see how the boys look after you. Four sons and God knows how many grandsons I've got, but only one daughter and a gem of a granddaughter.' To himself he added: No thanks to that stinking swine Leonard Kingston.

Some days I almost wish he would cross our door-step again. On second thoughts, best not. If the bugger did walk in, it would be a toss-up who got to him first. One thing would be for sure: his wedding tackle would never be in working order again.

Chapter 2

Carla worked for a Jewish family who owned several dry-cleaning businesses. At least that was how it had started out. Today, several shops later, the business had become much more upmarket. She had been taken on as an apprentice when she left school at the age of fourteen. However, it hadn't taken long for Mr and Mrs Harrison and their son Wally to realise that she could be very useful in so many ways.

To begin with, she had volunteered to sew missing buttons on to garments that had been brought into the shop for cleaning. Next she had mended a seam that had come undone on a pair of men's trousers. Now, four years later, she was kept busy doing repair jobs and had proved her worth by making uniforms for herself and the other girl she worked with. Mr

Harrison had provided the material, a good-quality navy-blue linen. Carla had been given a free hand as to the style. The skirt was pleated from the waist down to calf length; the dress had a plain round neck, long sleeves and a white collar made from heavy lace. The finishing touch was a line of pearl buttons down the front, plain but expensive-looking.

Time permitting, because the shop at Stockwell in South London was very well patronised, Carla was working on an evening cloak for Mrs Harrison: black velvet with a black sateen lining. Both bales of cloth had come into the shop from an unknown source. Mrs Harrison had also acquired a pair of gold link buttons, a beautiful touch which embellished the cloak perfectly.

Fred brought the van to a halt just around the corner from the shop. He jumped down on to the pavement and slid the passenger door back, then reached in to help Carla down on to the pavement. The look on his face was grim.

'What's wrong, Fred?' she asked.

He didn't answer, instead nodding towards where the newspaper man had his stall set out on the opposite corner of the road. A huge placard declared: GERMANY INVADES POLAND.

'Now tell me we are not on the brink of another war,' Grandad shouted at his sons as he folded his newspaper. It was no longer any good hoping that the trouble with Germany would blow over.

Sure enough, on Sunday 3 September, the whole Schofield family were gathered around Grandad's wireless as the announcement came loud and clear: 'Britain is now at war with Germany.'

Neighbours, old and young alike, poured into the street. Sirens blared out from the dockyards. There wasn't a woman that wasn't crying. Some had thrown their aprons up over their faces. Granny Blackshaw spoke for them all as she whispered, 'Our sons will have to go to fight like our husbands did in the last war. How many will be killed this time?'

Air-raid sirens sounded in many parts of Britain. They were all false alarms, but it was a grim reminder that in this coming war, civilians would be in the front line right from the beginning.

But unlike 1914, Britain in 1939 was better prepared for the nightmare that lay ahead. Every window of every house had to have blackout curtains, and on buses, trams and other forms of public transport, windows were heavily taped to prevent flying glass. The tiniest hint of light from the edge of a window prompted an angry shout of 'Put that light out!', with the possible consequence of a fine or prison sentence. If you weren't careful, folk might even become suspicious and assume that you were signalling to German aircraft.

Everyone was urged to grow their own food, whether it be on an allotment, in the garden or even in a window box. Ration books were already in use, and quantities would get smaller and smaller if the war went on too long. Feeding a family had become an ordeal.

The government offered every household in the big cities an Anderson air-raid shelter, to be erected in the garden. Many young children from the cities were evacuated to the country. It was sheer torture to watch the parents saying their goodbyes to these poor little mites. Far too often the strangeness of the countryside and the totally different way of life there made the arrangement an absolute catastrophe, and many families brought their children back home.

'If we're gonna die, then we'll all die together,' was a comment heard from many a mother's lips. That was exactly the way every member of the Schofield family felt. Come what may, they were going to stay together.

So far none of the Schofield men had received their call-up papers, but they were all well aware that it was only a matter of time.

At least there was the occasional ray of light in between the bad news put out over the radio. Some cinemas were still functional, and were advertising a movie that would run for three hours. The title was *Gone with the Wind*. An unknown English actress, Vivien Leigh, had been chosen for the much-envied part of Scarlett O'Hara, playing opposite Hollywood's leading man, Clark Gable.

Mrs Harrison had given Carla two pounds for the velvet cloak, and Carla decided that she and her aunts deserved a treat. She had queued up outside the cinema for three quarters of an hour, and when she reached the cash desk was told that if she wanted five tickets, the earliest day she could have them would be the first Monday in May – that was, in ten days' time.

'The date is fine,' Carla smiled, 'but please, what kind of seats are they, and how much will they cost?'

'Dress circle, third row back, and the cost will be half a crown each.'

Carla found a space along the wall and stood there carefully stowing the precious tickets in her bag. She was feeling quite pleased with herself, as she had expected them to be more expensive. She wasn't quite sure, but she thought the dearest seat in this cinema would normally be about two shillings; since this film ran for three hours, she was thrilled that the tickets had only cost her twelve shillings and sixpence.

What a wonderful evening that was! The five of them laughed and cried, and they weren't alone. This film was proving to be one of the most popular movies ever made.

Chapter 3

At night, after Carla had eaten her evening meal, she was picked up by Mr Harrison in his car.

'God alone knows how long it will be before there's no more petrol to be had, but it will happen eventually,' he complained as he drove her to his big house on the far side of Clapham Common.

Carla had proved herself to be a remarkable needle-woman, and Mr Harrison had recognised her worth. Having foreseen the shortages that were bound to come, he had bought up every bale of material he could lay his hands on, and turned two rooms in his family home into a workshop.

Carla had grasped the opportunity, designing and sewing garments for Mr Harrison's growing number of clients. It wasn't long before she was well aware that her boss was doing very nicely from the fruits of her labours. And she was profiting from the business too, with Mr and Mrs Harrison paying her a reasonable sum for each item they sold.

All good things must come to an end sometime. And reality hit the Schofield families with a vengeance. All four brothers had received their call-up papers. Carla was finding it hard to be brave. The women had decided that the railway station would be too crowded and the atmosphere far too gloomy for them to see their men off from there. So here they were, clustered around the bus stop.

'You'll be fine, you'll take care of each other,' Sid said, tightening his grip on Mary.

'Course you will. You have each other and we know you'll keep an eye on Grandad and our Carla.' Fred was still clutching Brenda's hand. It had come as a shock to him to receive his call-up papers. Working for the Royal Mail as he had since he was a young lad, he had hoped his job would have been classed as a reserved occupation. Neither Jack nor Albert was keen to leave their families either, but they knew where their duty lay.

Each woman was relieved when the bus arrived. It had been hard enough this morning for the children to say goodbye. None of them had wanted to go to school.

Hugs, kisses and pats on the back. 'I'll write to you all,' Carla promised.

Suddenly she felt dizzy. Her uncles would be gone. Mary, Brenda, Edna and Daisy had their own young boys to worry about. Things would be very different at home.

The bus was moving. The Schofield women stood amongst other wives and mothers, all of them waving courageously despite the fact that tears were streaming down their faces, as they wondered when they would see their men again.

Chapter 4

Five days later, a buff-coloured envelope dropped on to the front-door mat. On the back of it were stamped the words RECRUITMENT PAPERS ENCLOSED.

Carla turned the envelope over. It was addressed to Miss C. Schofield. This has to be a joke, was her first reaction as she took out the letter.

Please attend the recruitment centre at the Broadway premises, Chiswick, at 11 a.m. on Thursday 11 June 1940.

'Good gracious me! Carla exclaimed out loud.

Grandad did his best to keep a stiff upper lip when he heard the news, but his temper got the better of him as the day drew near, and he voiced his opinion to anyone who would listen, declaring that it was bad enough that all the young men were being called up, but to start now on young girls and even middle-aged women was a step too far.

Carla was giving herself a good talking-to as she brushed her long, thick hair, making it ready to wind into two plaits, which she would then coil and pin back neatly. Can't look too frivolous today, she told herself.

When she had finished, she poured a mug of tea and took it over to her grandad. Then she sat down on the floor with her own mug and leaned back against his legs.

'Edna is going to come in and sit with you this morning, and Daisy will be here for the afternoon. All four of them will be popping in and out, and they'll make sure you get a hot dinner.'

'For God's sake, gal, give it a rest. Yer only going for an interview. I'll be fine. I do all right when you're at work, don't I?'

Carla reached her arm backwards and pulled his head down until she was able to plant a kiss on his cheek. Then, getting to her feet, she wrapped her arms around his shoulders and hugged him close.

'I don't know what time I shall be home, but you behave yourself. Luv you.'

'Luv yer too, even though yer getting a bit lippy.'

She drained her mug and quickly made her way upstairs to fetch her coat. If she stayed there any longer, she'd end up in tears, and that would only serve to upset Grandad.

Carla arrived twenty minutes early for her interview and sat nervously in a waiting room that was bare of any comforts. She heaved a sigh of relief when a tall, well-dressed gentleman appeared and asked her to follow him.

The room they entered was vastly different from the waiting room. At the far end there was a raised platform, the centre of which held a massive desk. Carla was asked to sit down on a chair which had been placed facing the desk. As she did so, another gentleman and a lady came from the left-hand side of the platform and seated themselves behind the desk.

In turn the introductions were made. Mr Greenford was on the far left, Miss Coppard in the centre chair. Mr Rayner, the gentleman who had fetched her from the waiting room, completed the trio, and it was he who made the opening remarks.

'We need to ask you, Miss Schofield, whether you have any preference as to what war work you will be assigned to.'

Carla cleared her throat. 'I wasn't aware that it is obligatory for me to participate in any work related to the war effort.' She sounded a lot more sure of herself than she actually felt.

Miss Coppard smiled and said gently, 'Britain needs help from all able-bodied people within the age limit. Are you raising an objection?'

'Not at all,' Carla said quickly, 'but I'm not sure that I can help in any way.'

Miss Coppard had taken over. 'Several options are open to you. Nursing is one, but you would need a great deal of training for that, though there is auxiliary nursing, which would be grateful for your help. There's also farm work, munitions, or maybe you'd be interested in becoming a London bus conductor.' She paused, then suggested, 'Maybe it would be more helpful if we asked you how you earn your living now.'

Carla managed a little grin. 'I do a lot of sewing.'

'Would you be more explicit, please.'

'I am employed by Mr and Mrs Harrison, who own two dry-cleaning shops. To start off with I used to do small repairs to any of the garments that needed it. As time went on I progressed to making various garments. It all depends on what material Mr Harrison can lay his hands on.'

Mr Greenford had a huge smile on his face as he said, 'In that case, how does making uniforms for our forces strike you?'

Carla's head was swimming with questions, but she took a deep breath and thought for a moment before attempting to form her answer.

'You'd need a hefty great sewing machine to do that. The uniforms would all need a heavy cloth, and no ordinary machine could take on that kind of work.'

'You certainly know what you are talking about, Miss Schofield,' Mr Greenford said. 'Many manufacturers will be turning their factories over to the production of military uniforms, but there will not be many male operators available.'

Carla forced herself to smile before saying, 'So you're thinking of using women, but will they be experienced?'

'Yes, and that is where you might be very helpful. A few weeks acquainting yourself with the set-up here in Chiswick might help you to decide.'

'Oh, so I would be given some choice in this arrangement?' Carla asked cheekily.

That brought a smile to the faces of all three of the interviewers, and Mr Rayner murmured, 'Spoken like a true cockney.'

He didn't speak quietly enough for Carla to miss it. 'Too true I'm a cockney, through an' through, and if you were to ask my grandad, he'd tell yer you might find our equals if you searched long enough, but you'd never find our betters.'

No sooner were the words out of her mouth than she felt her cheeks flame up, but she had no need to worry. The examiners were laughing fit to bust. Mr Greenford was the first to regain his composure.

'Before you make any decision, you should view the premises that are up and running now, but you should also realise that the present arrangement was always meant to be temporary. The whole operation is scheduled to be transferred to Southend-on-Sea within the next few weeks.'

A lengthy silence fell, until Miss Coppard suggested

that she take Carla to another room, where coffee would be ready for them.

Carla heaved a sigh, wondering just what she was letting herself in for. One moment she was excited, then the next minute wary, as dozens of questions filled her head.

Would she be able to cope with such heavy work? How much training would be available? What kind of money would she be offered to do this essential war work? Most importantly, if the whole operation was going to be moving to Southend, surely that would mean that the workers would have to go too.

Carla's thoughts were still racing around in her head as she walked between the lines of sewing machines that had been set up in this Chiswick warehouse.

She wasn't sure which impressed her the most: the sewing machines, the like of which made her feel quite envious, or the well-dressed elderly gentlemen who were busy handling them. They all wore black pinstriped trousers topped with snow-white shirts and grey ties, which looked immaculate beneath their well-fitted black waistcoats.

'You look shocked,' said Maureen, the middle-aged woman who was showing Carla around. She smiled. 'I can read your thoughts,' she said. 'You're wondering where all these elegant gentlemen have come from? Am I right?'

'Well yes, that is exactly what is going through my mind. In some ways it all looks perfectly normal . . .'

She hesitated. 'And yet in other ways they seem out of place.'

'These gentlemen are all professional tailors,' Maureen said. 'Their work is well known and sought after worldwide. In their heyday they had premises in the West End of London, dressing rich men and even travelling abroad when commissioned.'

Carla had a million and one questions she badly wanted to ask, but caution warned her to be prudent. Surely these men had not been called up; they must have volunteered. She wondered if they would be going to the new premises in Southend. She smiled to herself. She could learn so much from professionals like these. The war wouldn't last for ever, and who knows, she might end up being a top-class dressmaker herself. Even dress royal ladies one day! Oh yeah, and pigs might sprout wings and fly, she mentally chided herself.

At the far end of the room, trestle tables had been set up and more gentlemen were cutting cloth with huge scissors, while bales of material were stacked against the wall, the colours representing every branch of the armed forces.

'I think you have seen enough for the time being.' Miss Coppard's head popped around the side wall. 'You are going to be treated to lunch now, Carla. I am sure you will be seeing Maureen again soon.'

Two weeks later, Carla had come around to accepting that she was to be working with these first-class tailors, at least for the time being. When the premises at Southend were declared ready, that would be a different story altogether. For the most part she was content and eager to learn, yet at the same time the sight of the various uniforms made her dreadfully sad. Another generation of young men in their prime were to be sacrificed to the horror of war.

Weeks turned into months, and still the move to Southend had not taken place. Yet Carla felt the time had not been wasted. She had learnt so much and had made some really good friends, with expert tailors always on the end of a phone should anything go wrong.

The country had struggled through 1940, but no sooner had 1941 begun than the Luftwaffe resumed the Blitz on London. On 24 May, HMS *Hood* was sunk off Greenland by a German ship, the *Bismarck*. Fred Schofield, Carla's eldest uncle, was amongst those killed. Carla was given two days off work to be with the family. It would take a lifetime for Brenda, Fred's wife, and his young son Joseph to come to terms with their loss. As for Carla, she thanked God for the fact that they still had each other.

Chapter 5

Carla had given up thinking about the move to Southend. It had been months now, and she was convinced she would still be working here in Chiswick when the war came to an end. As for everyone else involved in war work, it had become a way of life. Her workmates were a grand bunch of people who all helped each other no matter what needed doing. When the air raids over London were continuous night after night, Peggy Lewis insisted on taking Carla home with her. She lived just ten minutes' walk from the factory, and the entire Lewis family welcomed Carla with open arms. On Sundays, Carla would take Peggy home with her for the day.

This exchange of happy families was not to last for ever. Although it had taken much longer than anyone had anticipated to wind up the premises in Chiswick and arrange the move, by the end of 1941 everything was ready. The date set for departure was January 1942.

Before they left London, there was Christmas to be got through. Any celebrations there might have been were dampened by the news on 7 December of the Japanese attack on the US base at Pearl Harbor.

'Now that will bring the Americans into this war,' said Grandad wisely.

Carla felt she was setting out on an adventure. Never in all her years had she ventured far from the East End of London. Now she would be starting a new life in Southend. Was that what she wanted? Had she been given any choice?

Had any of the young lads who were fighting hundreds of miles away from home had a choice? she asked herself. How about the families, her own included? Not even a decent funeral for relations to attend. Once the war came to an end, there would probably be endless memorials erected in towns and villages, but would they serve to ease the pain?

For God's sake get on with packing your suitcase, Carla told herself. Southend wasn't a million miles away; she could get a train home every Sunday if she wished. And anyhow, she should give herself time to get used to the place. She did enough moaning about never going anywhere, and here she was, rail fare all paid, and going to live by the sea.

Real fresh salt air! It had to be better than the murky dockyard water.

The removal went well. An army lorry had called at the workers' homes, picking up their suitcases. That certainly made travelling much easier. Once on the train, the significance of the step they were taking hit everyone, and Carla was no exception. On arrival, the women were lined up on the platform whilst the men were taken to vans that were standing by to transport them to their digs. Members of the Women's Auxiliary Services were dishing out cards with the addresses of the places that had been assigned as lodgings for females.

Carla and Peggy took a quick look at their cards and then threw their arms around each other. 'We've been put together,' they both yelled. 'Yeah, with a Mrs Elsie Stevens, who has two children of school age,' Peggy read from the card. 'Don't say anything about a man being in the house, but suppose he's more than likely been called up,' she added.

Two gentlemen seemed to be in charge of the women. Miss Schofield and Miss Lewis were the first two names called out, and the girls stepped eagerly up to the front.

'Follow me, ladies, but make sure that you have every piece of your hand luggage. You are going in the first car because the house where you are being billeted is only about twenty minutes away.'

The car was waiting for them, the back door being held open by a jolly-looking woman. As soon as she spotted the girls, she called out, 'Come on, me dearies, we ain't got far to go and I'll lay you a tanner to a shilling Elsie Stevens will have her kettle on and we'll all be offered a cuppa, that's if she hasn't used up all her ration for this month. By the way, I'm Dot Collins, I work for the Women's Auxiliary Brigade.'

If the welcome they received as they stepped out of the car was anything to go by, then the two girls knew they were on to a good thing. Listening to Mrs Stevens talking, they both felt they weren't that far from London.

'Come on, me dears. I'm glad to see they've sent me a couple of healthy youngsters, 'cos your room is up on the third floor.'

Peggy made a face and muttered to Carla from the side of her mouth, 'Third floor? How big is the house, for Christ's sake?'

As their new home came into view, both girls gasped with surprise. It was a detached property with a big front garden, not the least bit like the streets of back-to-back terraces they were used to in London.

And it got better! The room they were sharing had two single beds and there was room to walk around even though several very large pieces of furniture were arranged against the walls.

'Dump yer stuff an' come down to the kitchen. I bet you're gasping for a drink, an' you've got the rest of the day to unpack and find yer way around.

I've been told by those in the know that none of you have to report to the factory today. Tomorrow will be soon enough, and from then on it'll be all go, so make the most of it while yer can.'

Having said her piece, Elsie Stevens left the girls alone, but she had got only halfway down the stairs when she stopped and yelled, 'Sorry, forgot t'tell yer, bathroom is down here on the first floor, but there's a pot under each of the beds in case you need to wee in the night.'

Carla and Peggy looked at each other, then burst out laughing. It took a few minutes for them to calm down, but when they did, they agreed that so far it looked as if they had fallen on their feet.

Carla opened the double doors to a massive ward-robe and, seeing the rows of empty coat hangers, started laughing again. 'Just how many clothes does this landlady think we've got? You can bet yer life we won't get any spare time to run anything up for ourselves, even if we had enough coupons for the cloth.'

The kitchen was an absolute dream. A scrubbed white-topped table stood in the centre of the room with six high-backed chairs, two of which were occupied by Dot Collins and Elsie Stevens. Elsie immediately got to her feet, urging the girls to sit down. 'Do either of you take sugar?' she asked.

'We've both learnt to do without,' Carla said, smiling.

'That's a relief. I hope you have your ration books

with you.' Both girls nodded as Elsie placed a plate of home-made fairy cakes on the table. 'Even my two children have learnt to do without sugar in their drinks, and that's how come I'm able to do a bit of baking. By the way, I have a boy and a girl. Edward is seven, and Rosie nearly six. I've already told the butcher that I'll be registering two extra ration books with him, so that should enable us to have a small joint for Sunday dinner. Anyway, drink your tea and have a cake, then maybe you'd like to take a walk down to the seafront. You won't be able to go on to the beach, though, as it's all cordoned off.'

Both girls jumped at the chance to go and look at the sea, but it didn't take long for Carla to realise that Southend was not at all as she remembered it from her childhood. The first time she had been there, she must have been about five years old. It was Easter Monday, a bank holiday, and Nan and Grandad had paid for all the family to have a chara-banc ride to see the lights.

There had been a long pier stretching out to sea, and Carla suddenly recalled how frightened she had been as she walked the length of it. The sea had been very rough, and she could see it churning around in the spaces between the boards. But there were so many lovely memories too. Ice-cream cornets, a ride on the dodgems, sticky candy floss. Cockles to eat off little dishes and some wrapped up ready to be taken home.

Now, though, the pier was all boarded up. Hardly

a shop was open for trade, and those that were had only a very small selection of goods for sale. 'Oh look,' Carla cried. 'The cockle sheds are still here. We must come down very early one morning and buy some. They always taste best when they are hot and fresh.'

Peggy made a face. 'Don't tell me you like cockles.'

'Course I do. You've never lived if you haven't tasted cockles.'

'We'd better take a few deep breaths while we're down here. Come tomorrow, when we start work in the new premises, I don't suppose we'll get much fresh air.'

Back at the house, Mrs Stevens' children were home from school. They were both friendly and polite, and it was a happy meal they all enjoyed as they got to know each other.

Carla and Peggy spent some of the evening unpacking their suitcases, and when they finally climbed into bed, they were thankful that the move had gone so well. At the same time, their minds were filled with apprehension as to what tomorrow was going to bring.

'We'll find out soon enough,' was Peggy's parting shot before she switched off the light.

Thirty workers in all had been transferred to Southend: twelve men and eighteen women. The men would mostly be doing the cutting of the cloth, and the girls were each allocated their own sewing machine. The very look of these machines marked them out as phenomenal; the equivalent of a Rolls-Royce motor car, as one man exclaimed loudly. There were several instructors dotted about, and it didn't take very long for the girls to get the hang of the machines. Once they had, each and every one of them realised what a privilege it was to be working on them.

As the needles purred, the girls talked amongst themselves about what would happen to them when the war was over. Carla had already decided that she wanted to set up her own business. With such teachers as the first-class tailors she had worked with in Chiswick, how could she go wrong? She had watched, listened and practised, and she could even cut cloth now.

A whole uniform was not beyond her, even if she was nowhere like as quick as the real tailors were. Some parts of a jacket still caused her problems, but as these gentlemen had reminded her time and time again, practice makes perfect.

Two months had flown by since Carla had left home. She received regular letters from her aunts and she always answered them straight away. The letters never contained any bad news, but Carla and Peggy regularly listened to the wireless with Mrs Stevens, and these past few days had been frightening. London was getting air raids day and night. 'Last night the Germans went for the docks,' the newsreader's voice informed them. 'The whole area is an inferno. Many buildings were hit, including the London Hospital, the gasworks and Woolwich Arsenal. The biggest fear is the threat of fire, incendiaries mixed with high explosives sending flames and dense black smoke high into the sky.'

Carla grabbed Peggy's hand and held on tightly, imagining that she could hear the noise and feel the heat.

Eight o'clock next morning found Peggy and Carla walking along the promenade.

'Did you manage to get any sleep?' Carla asked.

'A bit. I don't know about you, Carla, but my imagination runs away with me. God knows how those poor folk manage day after day.'

'Yeah, I know what yer mean. I was wondering, are we ever going to get any leave?'

'We should be about due for some, I should think, but there again, where would we go?'

'Home, of course. If our families have to put up with these air raids night after night, it wouldn't do us any harm to suffer for a few days.'

'That's true. Let's have a word and see if we have any joy.'

Everything had gone to plan, and Carla and Peggy were waiting on Southend railway station for a train that would take them up to Fenchurch Street in London. They had been advised to travel light, and that was proving to be good advice.

Reaching London, the train was stopped short of

its destination by police and two ARP wardens, and the passengers had to walk the rest of the way. They passed buildings that had had all their windows blown out, and in one case the front of a block of flats had completely disappeared, revealing the interior like an open-fronted doll's house. The air was thick with smoke and brick dust; it made the girls' eyes sting and soon they were both coughing. Policemen and wardens were busy everywhere doing their best to help any survivors.

'And where do you two young ladies think you are making for?' a warden asked Carla.

'I want to get to Tilbury Terrace – it's about five minutes' walk from the main docks – but my friend needs to get to Chiswick.'

'You are very optimistic,' the warden said. 'The docks took a bit of a bashing, though actually Tilbury was lucky: the pool was pretty full and that water saved many a life. Have you got any money on you?'

Carla was wary straight away. 'Why would you be asking that?'

'I am not after yer money, miss, but there's a cab rank just over the road, and if you know anything about London, you'll know that a cabbie can turn his cab on a sixpence, which serves him in good stead in times like terday. He could get you where you want to go, I'd take a bet on it.'

Both girls heaved a sigh of relief and Carla was falling over herself to say sorry for having doubted

33

the man. 'I think you suggested the best thing we can do, and I do thank you for your help.'

'Come along then, may as well finish what I've started. Hold on to each other and follow me, but keep your eyes on where you're putting yer feet. Don't want yer falling down a crater, do we?'

The taxi driver they found said that he was thinking about going home, calling it a day, and he lived near Tilbury himself. 'What about the other young lady?' he asked cheekily. 'Where would she like me t'take 'er?'

'Same place as me just for tonight, but perhaps we could book you for tomorrow morning to take her over to Chiswick.'

'Sufficient for the day. We'll take care of tomorrow if and when it comes.' He said the words seriously and at the same time made the sign of the cross.

The taxi drove past mounds of broken bricks and snaking hoses. Street after street looked more like an abandoned builder's yard. Then suddenly there they were! The row of terraced houses where her family all lived. True, several windows were boarded up, two chimney pots were leaning against the wall and the ground was surrounded by broken roof tiles, but what the hell, she'd made it. She was home.

There was no need to knock on the front door; it burst open and a crowd of women and boys rushed out on to the pavement. Tears mingled with smiles as they each in turn cuddled and kissed Carla. Peggy wasn't left out of the welcome either. Then they trooped inside and Carla gasped in amazement. The living room windows were boarded up, but pretty flowered curtains still hung each side of the blackout. The kitchen table was covered with a linen tablecloth, and a vase of fresh flowers was set in the centre. The sideboard too was a picture to behold. Dishes and plates of tempting food crowded the surface. Most importantly, Grandad was sitting upright in an armchair with a fluffy tartan rug covering his legs.

Carla dropped to her knees and took one of his hands between both of hers as she leaned forward to kiss his cheek.

'My God, I've missed you, pet,' he murmured, 'but you don't look the worse for wear. I thought it was some posh young lady coming in through the door.'

'Get on with you, Grandad, you still know how to make a girl feel good.'

'After all the trouble we've gone to, begging, borrowing and almost stealing, is nobody going to put the kettle on?' Brenda asked loudly.

Daisy took up the challenge. 'Let's all sit down and make a start on this food. We've got a few days to catch up on everyone's news.'

Mary had always been the quietest of the aunts, but now she turned to Peggy and asked, 'Was the journey all that bad?'

Peggy smiled. 'No, it was fine. The nightmare only began after we got off the train. How you have all managed to live from day to day with the air raids is beyond my comprehension. Carla and I regularly listen to the news, but even our imagination hasn't come close to the reality that we have seen in this last hour.'

'Yes,' we did take a beating last night, but you'd be surprised just how quickly the authorities get down to the clearing up. You must be anxious to see your own family.'

'Yes, I am, but it is kind of you to have me for tonight.'

'Well then, let's all get seated as best we can. Look, Daisy has made the tea, and thanks to all our neighbours and the local shopkeepers, who all know and love our Carla, between us we have scraped together a feast fit for you war workers.'

That was nothing short of the truth. There was plenty of corned beef but some real ham in the sandwiches, and big portions of cheese, which was something they rarely saw in Southend, as well as home-made cakes by the dozen. It was a long, noisy meal, but such a happy one, and all the boys were full of questions about Carla's new life.

For both girls it was wonderful to be home, but the three days of their leave flew past, and before they knew it, the girls were on their way back to Southend. Did the folk who lived there really appreciate how much safer their lives were? True, many German planes flew over and the ack-ack guns would open up on them, but it was London and other big cities that the Germans were after.

Being back at work kept them busy, but the thought of what they had seen and heard and the hardships that their loved ones were having to suffer made them sad. They could only pray that this dreadful war would quickly be brought to an end.

Chapter 6

It didn't take long for the girls to get back into their work routine. One morning, Carla was sitting at her machine when she heard a cheerful whistling and knew that she was about to have a visitor.

'Hiya, Skinny, how is your day progressing?'

'I'd get on a whole lot better if I didn't keep getting interruptions, and I do wish you wouldn't call me Skinny.'

'Well you have to agree, there isn't much flesh on your bones, but as the saying goes, the nearer the bone, the sweeter the meat.'

Carla couldn't help herself, she had to laugh. Besides, the more she got to know this young man, the greater the admiration she had for him.

Paul Robinson was six foot two inches tall. He had

a head of thick dark hair, really lovely deep brown eyes, a warm smile and an infectious laugh. When Carla had first met him, she had wondered why such a fine figure of a man was working here and hadn't been called up to join the forces. Then she noticed the steel brace around his left ankle, and the way he dragged his foot.

It was Peggy who found out more about him. He was twenty-three years old and before the war had been aiming to be an engineer. He was certainly a wizard when it came to machinery. Even these wonderful up-to-date sewing machines sometimes went wrong, or one of the girls would get their thread caught up, but not a single problem had arisen that Paul hadn't been able to rectify.

Carla was concentrating on a seam and was aware that Paul was saying something. She lifted the silver foot rest that held the needle in place, removed the cloth and leaned back in her chair. Had she heard him right? He was looking very pleased with himself.

'You're wondering how I found out that it's your birthday next week,' he said, grinning from ear to ear. 'A twenty-first can't be ignored. I have already had words with the owner of one of the decent hotels in the town and he has promised to do the very best he can. If he can't manage it, I am going to try for the church hall.'

For a moment Carla couldn't form an answer, then she managed to say, 'Why would you do that for me?'

'I'm doing it because I want to. Take your time, ask everybody that you would like to come and leave the rest to me.'

'There's a war going on and you are preparing a do because it's my twenty-first birthday?' She truly did feel flabbergasted.

'That's it in a nutshell,' he agreed, still with a great grin on his face. 'All you have to do is write out the invitations and see if you can rustle up a party frock, because this is one occasion when I don't want to see you wearing those trousers. I'm sure Peggy will help you.'

'Too right I will,' Peggy answered. 'It is a wonderful idea, and when Carla gets her breath back she'll be as pleased as I am. I think all of us deserve one night when we can try and forget this ruddy war.'

'Thanks for your vote of confidence,' said Paul. 'I'll leave the pair of you to get on with your work now, but we'll talk later.'

When the girls got home that evening, Peggy outlined to Elsie what Paul had in mind for Carla's birthday. Teddy and Rosie listened, then asked as one, 'Will we be allowed to come?'

'Of course you will,' Carla quickly assured them.

Their mother, however, was playing it cautiously. 'There's quite a lot of things that have to be sorted out before anyone can be invited, but if you are both good, I shall do my best to take you with me on the day.'

'Oh, so you do believe it will take place?' Peggy asked.

The three women looked at each other and grinned, but it was Peggy who came up with what they were all thinking.

'Everyone has had to bear hardships and losses since this war began, but there isn't a man or woman who hasn't tried to do their bit in one way or another. And that goes for all of us. How long since you've seen your husband, Elsie? And you've opened up your home to us war workers. Most of us here have had to leave our families, and it wasn't from choice. So if we take an evening off, do our best to forget the war just for a few hours, no one can blame us. I think it's wonderful of Paul Robinson to offer to fix it up, and the best way we can repay him is to enjoy the evening.'

Peggy bent down to the children's level before saying, 'Edward and Rosie, you have to be there or Carla will want to know why. After all, you are letting us share your house and we love you for that.' She lowered her voice. 'We shall have to practise singing "Twenty-one today, twenty-one today, Carla's got the key of the door 'cos she's twenty-one today."'

That made both children laugh.

'Will someone give her twenty-one bumps?' Teddy whispered the question into Peggy's ear.

'I think we shall have to wait and see,' she answered, but the very thought had brought a smile to her face. At that moment her mind was full of the fact that it was Paul Robinson who had started the ball rolling, and Carla was deluding herself if she thought he was just being friendly.

The news spread like wildfire. Everyone was enthusiastic, and Paul was getting offers of help from all sides. It was really amazing. Great care was taken that nothing was mentioned when Carla was about. Although she was aware that Paul had been serious about giving her a birthday party, not a soul wanted to discuss the plans with her, and they certainly weren't going to let her become involved with any of the arrangements.

The party was to take place on the evening of Carla's birthday, which was a Saturday. Paul had decided that the local church hall would be a better venue than the hotel he had first proposed. With everything arranged, all Carla had to think about was what she was going to wear. Ten days before the party, she and Peggy sat down with Elsie to plan their outfits for this special do.

Elsie had been to a wedding a couple of years ago and had splashed out on a navy blue and white floral dress and matching coat. Now she tried it on and gave it a twirl; the very full skirt flared out and both onlookers exclaimed their approval, Carla adding, 'I've always thought that navy blue is so much smarter than black. Would you agree to me letting the hem of the skirt down, perhaps even lengthening it? I could probably use some of the jacket for material.

A full-length skirt will look so much more classy, especially if there is to be dancing. Anyway, do you have a decent pair of stockings to wear with a short skirt? Or were you thinking of asking one of us to paint your legs?'

Peggy burst out laughing. 'Wouldn't be the first time I've done that, though it's never proved to be much of a success.'

'Well, there you are then. Beneath a long skirt you can wear a pair of ankle socks . . . which brings us to the question of shoes.' Carla had a smug look on her face as she said these words. Both she and Peggy loved dancing, and they had each brought a pair of party shoes with them from London. This would be the first opportunity they'd had to wear them.

Elsie admitted that she had a pair of silver sandals packed away at the back of her wardrobe. 'And if you're sure it won't be too much trouble, I would love you to make me a full-length skirt,' she said to Carla.

'No trouble at all. I know you have a hand sewing machine in your front room. Does it work?'

'Yes, I used it last week to turn a pair of bedsheets sides to middle.'

Carla heaved a sigh. If only they could use the machines at work. Still, she chided herself, even a hand sewing machine would save a lot of time.

'We shall work wonders, Peggy and I, you'll see. I am truly looking forward to this party now, and we three shall be well turned out on the night.'

Now it was Carla and Peggy who had to decide

what they were going to wear. If they had been at home, it wouldn't have been any problem; both girls would have found something suitable in their wardrobes. In the end they settled on cutting up a couple of silk nightdresses that they had never worn. Peggy's was a pale blue and Carla's a lovely peach colour that went well with her auburn hair. A couple of hours of hand sewing while Elsie rummaged through her button box to find enough pretty glass buttons, and each girl now had a beautiful long-sleeved blouse. Two full-length skirts were now needed.

'I'll tell you what' – Elsie was halfway out of the room when she called out over her shoulder – 'I've got some material I bought to make blackout curtains, but then I changed my mind and used what the government had provided. I won't be long. I know where it's packed away.'

The girls wrinkled their noses at each other. 'Going to a do, the first since God knows when, and all we've got to wear will be a skirt made out of blackout material!' Carla protested jokingly.

'Let's wait an' see what Elsie comes up with,' Peggy said, grinning.

'Well I'm blowed,' she muttered as Elsie dumped a long, narrow parcel on the floor. One end had burst its wrapping and the colour of the material could clearly be seen. In the main it was a very dark grey, but there were flecks of gold-coloured thread woven through it. By now both girls were on their knees, tearing away at the brown paper.

'Jesus, where on earth did you get this from?' Carla sounded just as flabbergasted as Peggy.

'Hammersmith wholesale market, actually,' Elsie said. 'Stan took me up one weekend, and almost everything the man had on the stall was dirt-cheap.'

'Wonders will never cease,' Carla declared.

Peggy and Elsie began to slowly unroll the material, and the more they uncovered, the wider the smiles on the girls' faces grew.

Peggy grabbed a pencil and started drawing sketches for two differently styled long evening skirts. Carla leaned over her shoulder.

'Don't forget I'm a little taller than you. I would still like a slit up the side, but not too high.'

'I'm glad you said that, because I'm going to have the slit at the back of my skirt.' With that comment, Peggy burst out laughing.

'Now what's tickled you?' Carla asked.

'I was thinking that under normal circumstances we wouldn't be seen dead going to a dance wearing almost the same skirt.'

'Sign of the times, eh?' Carla said. 'Let's hope we live to tell the tale.'

Chapter 7

With still more than a week to go before Carla's birthday, there was a bit of excitement one morning when the girls arrived for work. A minibus was parked across the entrance to the building, and as Peggy and Carla walked into the staffroom to hang up their coats and put on their overalls, they were met by six middle-aged ladies.

'Hallo, are you here to start work?' Carla asked.

'Yes, we are,' a tall, dark-haired lady answered, and another, older woman added, 'But we're not here to use sewing machines like you do. We hand-make medals.'

Both Peggy and Carla thought that they had not heard right, but it was Peggy who lightened the tone. 'Don't tell us the government are handing out medals before this blessed war is over.'

The women laughed, and one said, 'Ours not to reason why . . .'

'Have you been billeted locally?' Peggy wanted to know.

The older lady spoke up again. 'We all live locally, and some of us have been doing this work for years.'

'We're all hoping that maybe those in charge believe the war is nearing its end, and they will be handing out medals left, right and centre to all who have served their country.'

Another woman sniffed. 'Stocking up, more like. Much better to be safe than sorry.'

Mr Kingston, the manager of the department where Peggy and Carla worked, knocked hard on the staffroom door. 'Are you two young ladies intending to do any work today?'

'We're just coming, Mr Kingston,' Carla called out.

Quickly they donned their overalls and wished their new comrades the best of luck, but as they walked towards their sewing machines Carla couldn't resist saying, 'Producing medals prematurely, that's what my grandad would call putting the cart before the horse.'

It was Saturday morning, and with only a week to go to the birthday party, the girls were going shopping.

Elsie had made toast and placed it in the oven to keep warm. She was scrambling some dried egg when Carla and Peggy came into the kitchen.

'That's fresh tea in the pot. Help yourselves and

pour one for me, please. I thought I had got used to this dried egg, but I don't think it has whisked up at all well today,' Elsie complained as she placed a plate of scrambled egg on toast in front of each of them.

'Looks all right to me,' Carla assured her.

In fact the dried egg wasn't very nice at all, but far be it from either of them to say anything. Elsie did so much for them, and most of the time she worked wonders. No matter how short the rations were, she always made sure they never went hungry.

'Elsie, are you coming to the shops with us this morning?' Peggy asked between mouthfuls.

'Nice of you to ask me, and with me two kiddies gone to Saturday-morning pictures, I'm only too happy to share your company.'

'Silly question, I know,' Carla grinned, 'but has either of us got any coupons left, or any sweet ration?'

'I haven't touched the kiddies' sweet ration for this week, so we'll see what Mr McCarthy's got to offer. Would be nice if I could give Teddy and Rosie a bar of chocolate.' Elsie sighed. 'This war has brought so much sadness to families. My two write regular to their dad, but they don't ever seem to want to talk about him. They know he is in the Royal Navy and that's about it.'

'Are we walking or catching the bus into town?' Peggy wasn't known for her patience.

'We'll walk in and get the bus home, I think,' decided Elsie. 'You never know, we might be loaded down with shopping.'

'Yeah, and pigs might fly,' Carla laughed. 'Sounds daft, doesn't it? We both earn good money, yet there's not much in the shops for us to buy.'

'We have our war bonds, and come the time when we can cash them in, we'll have a field day. Come on, let's get going and see what is on offer today.'

It was a bright, clear morning and they had got within sight of the main shopping area when they heard the drone of aircraft and looked up to see what appeared to be dozens of planes. As there was no anti-aircraft fire, for a second they thought they were RAF planes, until they saw the German markings. It seemed as if everyone in the street suddenly realised that this was the real thing. All at once women began to scream, gathering their children close and running for all they were worth as the air-raid warning sirens sounded loud and clear.

'Get into the shelters!' the air-raid wardens were ordering, as two trucks drew into the kerb loaded with Civil Defence men.

Elsie was praying that her children would be safe in the cinema; nevertheless, she didn't panic but ushered Carla and Peggy into the relative safety of the covered market.

'We've had dozens of air-raid sirens going off in the last year,' she told them. 'It isn't places like here that the Germans want to drop their bombs. You've seen it for yourselves: it's the docks and the City of London, or else airfields and ships.'

Despite her soothing words, she couldn't help

thinking that too many warnings had gone off here in Southend. At first, people had dived for the shelters, but time had lulled them all into a false sense of security.

'Let's see if the café has any coffee today,' Elsie suggested as the noise from outside died down and they found an empty table.

Carla was as white as a sheet as she thought about how these air raids were a daily occurrence for her family back in the East End. She said a silent prayer that they would all be safe.

'We're in luck,' Elsie called from where she was standing by the counter. 'There is coffee today, though it's only bottled Camp coffee. Do you want that or tea?'

With one voice the girls said, 'We'll try the coffee.'

Elsie came back with a tray on which there were three cups of coffee and a spare saucer holding six saccharine tablets. 'Mrs Mountney said she is sorry they don't have any sugar; they've to go another week before they get the next ration.'

'And nothing to eat,' Peggy moaned. 'I could murder a lovely jam doughnut.'

'You and the rest of the country,' Elsie grinned. 'We all thought things might have got a bit better since the Yanks arrived, but it must be the big cities where they are stationed, 'cos we've not seen hair nor hide of them yet.'

They drank their coffee and had a good natter. When they'd drained every drop, they got up to go.

As soon as they came out into the street, their nostrils were assailed by the smell of burning, and the air was thick with dust. 'No one has been hurt,' an air-raid warden assured everybody; the college had caught some damage and their playing field was the worse for wear, but the Germans weren't going to waste their bombs on Southend.

Heaving a great sigh, Elsie said, 'Shall we go home, or do you still want to look in the shops?'

'Surely we aren't going to let our whole day be spoilt?' Peggy said.

'I doubt we'll be able to get through the high street,' Elsie argued.

'Then we'll find a detour,' Peggy declared.

Their determination paid off. As they came up to the main street, they looked across and saw that the doors to Mr McCarthy's shop were wide open. McCarthy's home-made sweets were a delight that most local folk had grown up with, and he was fond of saying to his many customers that no German was going to put him and his missus out of business.

'So who's the lucky girl who's going to have a birthday party?' Margaret McCarthy asked as soon as they entered the shop.

'Will you and Mr McCarthy be coming along?' Elsie asked.

'We'd love to pop in, wish the young lady all the best, but I think we shall have to play it by ear,' said Mr McCarthy. 'Food won't be a problem, from what me and the missus have heard; no one will come empty-handed.'

'It's the music I'm looking forward to,' Margaret said. 'Our eldest daughter tells us that the Boys' Brigade is going to be playing.'

Carla was quietly shaking her head.

'You don't look very pleased,' Mr McCarthy said. 'Like to tell me what is worrying you?'

'To be honest, Mr McCarthy, I'm overwhelmed. So many people offering to contribute, folk that don't even know me, and yet they are going all out just so that I can have a birthday party.'

'Not any old birthday,' Mr McCarthy laughed. 'Twenty-one is a real landmark. With you living here doing war work while all your family are in London, well, it's the least we can do. Besides, it's odds on that we locals will enjoy the get-together just as much as you will.'

Carla's eyes were brimming with unshed tears as she murmured her thanks, and her heart was bursting with love and appreciation. She was a complete stranger to this seaside town, but from day one each and every person that she had come into contact with had shown her kindness.

'You'll see, Carla, it will be a night to enjoy, and remembered by every person, young and old, as a wonderful time spent with friends.' Now Carla could not help herself; she let the tears trickle down her cheeks as Margaret McCarthy put her arms round her and held her close.

'Break it up, you two, you'll drive my customers away.' Leonard McCarthy was grinning, but his heart was touched. This lass should be at home with her own folk for her special day. But there again, he chided himself, the whole world was in turmoil, with so many young men and women separated from their loved ones. And who could say when they would see them again? Pulling himself together sharply, he turned to Elsie and held out three small parcels. 'I've put a few bits and pieces together for young Teddy and Rosie, and one pack is for you three.'

'Oh thanks ever so much, Mr McCarthy.'

'Wait a moment,' Mrs McCarthy called as she leaned over the counter. 'These are my little gift to you.' She handed Elsie a white linen bag, and as Elsie felt the lumpy contents, she knew she was holding some of Mrs McCarthy's home-made humbugs.

Hugs and kisses all round, and then the three of them were back out in the street. Peggy sniffed as they neared the open-air market. 'Tell me I am not dreaming,' she said.

'I don't think you are,' said Carla. 'I can smell it too. Let's run before my belly starts to rumble.'

The fish and chip shop was indeed open, with a queue forming outside. The two women in front of them were middle-aged and overweight, and jolly too.

'Seems some farmers have delivered a few sacks of spuds, so we'll probably get a bag of chips each even if there's no bloody fish,' said the elder of the two.

'Thank God for small mercies,' Carla grinned.

After a short wait, the three reached the counter, behind which stood an elderly man and two young girls who appeared to be twins. All three wore spotless white overalls.

'Sorry, me darlings,' the man said, 'we ain't got any fish today but we 'ave got chips an' a saveloy or chips and a sausage.'

'Mister, what's the difference between a sausage and a saveloy?' It was a lad of about sixteen who had called out the question from further back in the queue, and when the girls turned to look at him, he gave them a saucy grin and stuck his thumbs up in the air.

'Lad, the difference will be whether I serve you or not, so wait yer turn and we'll see when you get to the counter.'

Peggy spun the man a good yarn about their landlady and her two children and how their father was away in the Royal Navy, and how she and Carla were billeted with this lady because they had been sent down here from London to do war work.

'All right, me darling, enough of the bloody sob story. If I've 'eard yer right, that's three adults and two kiddies you're wanting a dinner for. Be all right if I give yer some of each?'

'Yes please,' they all replied with beaming smiles on their faces.

'Ain't got much paper to wrap them up in, but I'll pack them all in a cardboard box.'

'That will suit us fine,' they agreed.

'Blimey!' Elsie let the word out the minute they were outside the shop. 'The kids will be over the moon. Sweets from Mr McCarthy and sausage and chips for their dinner. They'll start thinking the war is over.'

'Shall we go straight home? Carla asked, using both arms to hold the box of food out in front of her.

'I think so,' Peggy said. 'Can't wander around the shops lugging that.'

'The sooner we get that food out and on to some dishes the better,' Elsie agreed happily.

Later in the day, when the table had been set and the children were home from the pictures, it was a contented gathering that sat down to have their dinner. For at least an hour, all thoughts of the country being at war were pushed aside.

Later still, when the children were ready for bed, their mother produced the small parcels Mr McCarthy had sent for them. The sweets were the finishing touch, though the children knew by now that it was best to eat only a few and leave some for tomorrow.

Elsie sighed heavily as she tucked the two children into bed. It had been a strange day, starting off with the air-raid warning and finishing so pleasantly thanks to the generosity of friends and neighbours. As she turned off the bedroom light and made her way downstairs, it was her turn to send up a prayer: 'Please God, let the leaders of all countries get together and make their peace. Too many young men have already died, and this war is not going to solve anything.'

Chapter 8

Carla's birthday had arrived. The whole of Saturday morning was spent going to and fro between the house and the church hall.

Amazement was the only way to describe the look on Carla's face when she, Peggy and Elsie first entered the hall. Elderly men were standing on stepladders hanging streamers and banners around the walls. It seemed that dozens of women were there too, all wearing pinafores. Cut flowers were one of the shortages of the war; they were still grown in some parts of the country, but there was no petrol for the transport of such luxury items. Fortunately, there was no lack of flowers for Carla's party. Two women were standing at a trestle table making beautiful arrangements from home-grown blooms and plenty of greenery. At another table several women were laying food out on large glass plates and then securely covering them with damp tea cloths.

Carla stood there open-mouthed as she struggled to take it all in.

'Happy birthday, my child.'

She turned quickly to see Father Jonathan standing behind her. She had spoken to the priest only twice before when she had attended a Sunday service with Elsie, and now she felt awkward. She took a deep breath before saying, 'Thank you for allowing us to use your church hall.'

'It is I who should be thanking you, my dear. Just look around you. So many folk are sharing your birthday and looking so happy. I am sure it will be a good day for a lot of people.'

'Well, thank you again. I hope you will look in this evening, perhaps have a glass of wine.'

'I shall do my best. In any case, you have a lovely evening.'

'I will, Father.'

Carla made her way to the kitchen, which was at the end of the hall. Having pushed the swing door open, she hesitated before she entered. There were so many women all working away, some seated at the table arranging food on fancy plates, others bending over the huge ovens, which were discharging the most gorgeous smells.

'All this activity, and all for you.' Peggy came smiling across the room. 'I have had orders to get you out of here, to take you home and see that you put your glad rags on ready for this evening.'

'I have been given the same orders,' Elsie laughed as she came over from the other side of the room. 'So gather yer bits together, Peggy, and let's get her home.'

Twenty minutes later, Elsie put the key into her front door and stepped quickly back. The doormat was covered in letters and cards. The three of them bent to pick them up. Carla's eyes were brimming with tears as she recognised her young cousins' handwriting, and one huge envelope that bore her grandad's scrawl. It was all too much for her. She gathered her post and went up to her room, where she collapsed on the bed and cried her eyes out.

Later she went to the bathroom and washed her face and hands. Looking at herself in the mirror, she gave herself a good talking-to. She had nothing to cry about. She had a good home here with Peggy and Elsie, and she even enjoyed the work she did.

A tap on the door had Carla grabbing a towel and rubbing hard at her face. She opened the door and Peggy held out her arms to her, and for a minute or two the pair of them stood on the landing and hugged each other.

They heard Elsie coming up the stairs and straightened themselves up.

'There are two ladies downstairs who have come with a suggestion. I think you should both come down and hear what they have to say.'

Two friendly-looking women were sitting at the kitchen table.

'I'm Alice and this is Kay, my next-door neighbour.' Everybody smiled and said hallo to each other. 'We've come with a proposition,' Alice continued as Kay nodded her agreement. 'Most of the women that have been helping in the hall today have small children, and rather than leave them out of the party, we suggest that they come with their mothers at about three o'clock, have a nice tea and play a few games, then go home at about six. Then the adults can sit down to eat. Would that be all right with you, Carla?'

'Most certainly,' Carla answered quickly. 'Will the mothers be able to come back for the evening?'

'Some will. I believe they have drawn up a roster, so we can safely say that no child will be left on their own.'

'I think that is very sensible,' Carla agreed.

'Good,' said Alice, looking pleased. 'We'll leave you to get ready and see you later on.'

The next few hours were chaotic. All three of them wanted a bath, and they drew lots as to who went first before the hot water ran out. Afterwards, Peggy sat in her dressing gown in front of a large mirror that Elsie had produced from under the stairs. Carla had heated a pair of tongs and carefully set Peggy's hair. Then it was Elsie's turn. Much easier for Carla, because Elsie's hair was very thick and naturally curly.

Carla had refused an offer from both of them to set her hair. She preferred to do her own. She leant forward and allowed her long tresses to hang loose. When it was dry, she plaited some of it to make a topknot.

Next, they all put a pretty-coloured varnish on their nails, and rubbed cream on their hands. They helped each other with their make-up and had a dab of Elsie's expensive perfume.

Finally it was time for them to put on their party clothes.

Elsie was the first to be ready, and the gasp of surprise that rose, even from the children, really did gladden her heart. Carla had made a wonderful job of turning the skirt of Elsie's two-piece into a full-length one, with a three-inch layer of creamy lace set into the material about three inches above the hem.

Neither Carla nor Peggy could quite believe that Elsie's blackout material had been transformed into expensive-looking skirts, or how they had managed to produce such lovely blouses from the two nightdresses.

Their shoes got the biggest smiles, as all three of them pointed their feet out to reveal that they were wearing silver sandals.

Rosie looked adorable in a pretty pink party dress and had sparkly slippers on her feet. Teddy was resplendent in long trousers, with a velvet waistcoat over his pale blue shirt. Elsie beamed at them proudly.

'Get your coats and let's get going. You children are to have your tea at about three o'clock, and then there will be time for a few games.'

When they arrived at the church hall, Teddy pushed open the doors, and his and Rosie's cries of delight made all the hard work that had gone into the making of this party well worth the effort.

Several small boys came running to greet Teddy, and soon Rosie was surrounded by a circle of prettily dressed little girls. It wasn't long before the rafters were ringing with children's laughter. Half a dozen men had taken on the job of organising the games, and they made sure that before long, every child in the hall had won a prize.

When it was time for the children to sit up at the table and have their tea, the sight was almost unbelievable. Tiny sandwiches, scones and jam, small fancy cakes and then tinned fruit and ice cream. Rationing was so tight – where on earth had all the food come from?

All too soon it was six o'clock, and parents were helping their children on with their hats and coats. Elsie had decided that she was going to go home with Teddy and Rosie but not return for the evening. As she left, two women handed her a cardboard box, saying, 'We've packed you a really nice meal, so once the children have gone to bed you will be able to enjoy it. One of the men has put a small bottle of wine in for you as well.'

Elsie was too choked up to say anything.

Once all the children had gone, the long tables were swiftly cleared and laid up again for the adults to have their meal. Peggy was helping out in the kitchen, but Carla had been ordered to stay away from the preparations, and she was beginning to feel like a fish out of water.

A tap on her shoulder had her turning sharply, and she almost fell into the arms of Paul Robinson. 'Happy birthday, Carla,' he said with a smile.

For a moment Carla felt puzzled. Why would an attractive man like Paul Robinson waste his time on her? He was well educated, came from a moneyed family, she had no doubt. She was a cockney from the East End of London. What did he see in her?

While her head was buzzing with these thoughts, Paul bent down so that his face was almost level with hers and very gently placed a kiss on her cheek. She didn't believe what was happening, but it felt so right.

'Sorry if I startled you,' he said, 'but every girl deserves a kiss on her birthday. I was wondering if you might let me sit next to you at the meal.'

Carla's pulse was jumping. 'Paul . . .' was all she managed to say. He leaned forward again and touched his lips to hers.

They were interrupted by the sound of a gong and a man's voice saying, 'Ladies and gentlemen, will you please take your seats at the table.' Soon everyone was seated, and then another elderly gentleman asked, 'Would you please all stand for the first toast of the evening. Please raise your glasses and drink to our dear friend Carla, who is twenty-one today.'

A lady seated at the piano struck up a few chords, and then everyone was singing 'Happy Birthday to You'.

That set the mood for the rest of the evening. The food was marvellous, the company great, and all sad thoughts of the war were put to one side for just a few hours. There was singing and dancing, and a good time was had by all, until the piano began the final song and everyone in the room stood up and linked hands to form a circle. One man made his way to the middle and called out, 'Let's dedicate this last tune to absent friends, and to all our brave young men who are so far from home.'

No one needed a second bidding. The hall rang with raised voices, the top notes reaching the rafters as they sang 'Auld Lang Syne'.

As the last notes died away, Carla moved into the centre of the room and a hush fell over her guests.

'I cannot begin to thank each and every one of you who has so kindly contributed to making my birthday such an outstanding one.'

She couldn't say another word. Her eyes were brimming, and she wasn't the only one in the room who was thinking of loved ones.

As Carla and Peggy put on their coats, Paul came over to where they were standing.

'I will see the two of you home safely,' he offered.

'Oh, there are at least six women who live close to Elsie's house and we've already agreed to face the blackout together, but thank you for the offer,' Carla said.

He caught her arm as she turned away. 'I have really enjoyed your company, Carla, and I hope you have enjoyed your birthday. There are things I would like to say to you, so if I have to forgo the pleasure of your company right now, will you consider letting me take you out one evening?'

Carla looked flustered, and Paul quickly added, 'You don't have to decide right now. I'll see you at work, and you can give me your answer then. Safe journey home, take care and I shall see you on Monday.'

Chapter 9

Carla sat up and stretched her arms above her head. Peggy had gone out for a walk with Elsie and the two children, but not before she had brought Carla a cup of tea in bed. Now she was having a lazy morning. In her mind she was going over and over the events of yesterday. In so many ways it had been a wonderful day. But then, there was nothing about her life that gave her cause to grumble. True, she had been uprooted from her home to do war work, but she was well aware that what she was learning here was going to stand her in good stead when this ruddy war did finally come to an end.

Of course she still missed London and every member of her family, but she had so many blessings to count. Being billeted with Elsie Stevens had been a godsend. They all got on splendidly. There were no arguments over household bills; everyone paid their share and did their bit around the house.

'Ah well,' she said aloud, 'I think it is time I got up and got myself washed and dressed, and it wouldn't hurt if I started to do the vegetables for our Sunday dinner before Elsie and Peggy get back with the kiddies.'

By midday, Carla had finished the vegetables and was thinking of the children enjoying the sunshine in the park. The beach was still out of bounds, more wire and padlocks than ever, almost as if the council were expecting the Germans to attempt an invasion. As she pushed her chair back and took the saucepan of shredded cabbage to the sink to cover it with cold water, the front doorbell rang. It wasn't like Elsie to forget her key, Carla thought as she walked up the long passage to the door.

When she threw it open, her heart came into her mouth and stinging tears filled her eyes.

'Oh my dear God,' she managed to exclaim before she spread her arms wide and embraced Edna and Daisy. All three women were now shedding tears, and yet their faces were wreathed in smiles. Not a word was uttered for a long moment, and then they all started to talk at once.

'What are you doing here?'

'Oh Carla, we could only afford for two of us to come, and we couldn't leave Grandad with all the boys, yet we felt we had to see you for your birthday, so we drew lots and me and Edna won,' Daisy explained.

'After travelling all the way from London, are we to spend the rest of the day on the doorstep?' Edna was trying to put a foot into the hallway but had not released her hold on Carla.

Once they had reached the kitchen and Edna and Daisy had laid down the many parcels they were carrying and taken off their coats, Daisy took charge. 'Let's get the bloody kettle on and a pot of tea made. We've brought tea with us just in case your rations had run out. We were on Fenchurch Street railway station at a quarter to six this morning and the blasted train wasn't able to leave until nearly eight, God knows why.'

Eventually they sat down with a cup of tea in front of each of them, but they never stopped talking, questions tossed back and forth across the table. They were so engrossed in their conversation that they didn't hear the front door opening, and were surprised when Peggy, Elsie and the children burst into the kitchen. Introductions were made, and Peggy hugged Daisy and Edna, and finally everyone settled down again. 'We're only here for the day,' Daisy explained to Elsie, 'but you have no need to worry about feeding us. When our friends and neighbours got to hear that the two of us were going to visit Carla, gifts came from all quarters. For starters we have brought a cooked ham, which will go well with all the vegetables Carla has prepared for lunch.'

Home-made cakes and all sorts of goodies were produced from the many parcels that Daisy and Edna had brought. There was even something for Rosie and Teddy: a bag of boiled sweets for each of them and a small bar of Nestlé milk chocolate. Grandad had saved his sweet ration especially for the two little children who were helping to keep his only granddaughter safe.

Afterwards, suggestions of going for a walk were pushed aside because the train back to London was due to leave at a quarter past seven. The afternoon passed swiftly. Tales of what was going on in London were told by the dozen. A detailed description of Carla's birthday party was given, more presents were delivered and opened, and the time just flew.

The clock struck six thirty, and five women and two children set out for the railway station. Everyone wanted to be with Daisy and Edna right up to the very last minute.

The shrieking whistle gave warning that the London-bound train was approaching, and Carla told herself she was not to cry. Despite all their resolutions, however, there was not a dry eye to be seen as Daisy and Edna climbed into the carriage and came forward to lean out of the window.

'Don't forget to hug Grandad for me, and tell him that I love him and that I shall see him soon,' said Carla, the tears streaming down her face.

They stood waving until the train was out of sight, then Elsie turned to Carla and Peggy. 'Well, that's two consecutive days that have turned out to be absolutely brilliant. Dare we hope for a third?'

Carla was quick off the mark. 'Pushing your luck, I'd say, but we can always live in hope. Come on, kids, let's get home and see what's on the wireless.'

'Oh do we have to?' Teddy wasn't at all pleased. 'Before we have to go to bed, will you play a game of Ludo with us?'

'Of course I will. Now hold my hand and we'll see how quickly we can make it home.'

They spent the evening playing board games with Rosie and Teddy, but Carla wasn't sorry when it was time for them all to say goodnight and head for their beds. She could tell by her deep breathing that Peggy had soon got off to sleep, but she herself was finding it far more difficult.

Her aunts had told her that she was looking stronger and more beautiful than they'd ever seen her. They had insisted that her long auburn hair was still her crowning glory and that being twenty-one certainly suited her. All of that had been very nice to hear, and she did know that this war work was an experience that was going to stand her in good stead for the future.

However, she was a Londoner, a true cockney, born within the sound of Bow bells, and her family were embedded deep in her heart. She missed them all so much, and felt guilty that she had upped and left them. But did she have any choice? she asked herself.

Oh, this bloody war had so much to answer for!

She pulled the bedclothes over her head but she couldn't shut out the images of her family. Once the war came to an end, she would be back in London and would help them all in whatever way possible. And her beloved grandad would be her number one priority.

Having settled all of that in her mind, Carla was at last able to relax. The last two days beggared description, and with that happy thought she closed her eyes and went to sleep.

Chapter 10

The war dragged on throughout 1943. In June 1944, hopes were raised when the Allies invaded Normandy. Yet the terrible conflict was to continue for almost another year. It wasn't until May 1945 that the longed-for words came over the wireless, and every newspaper carried the headline: GERMANY SURRENDERS UNCONDITIONALLY. Winston Churchill was cheered by crowds on his way to the House of Commons. Finally the defeat of Germany had been brought about.

In Southend, all staff had been asked to stay on at the factory for the time being. Nothing had as yet been decided, and there was to be an open meeting in two days' time. Carla and Peggy, though, had both made up their minds. Come what might, they were going home to spend some time with their families before making any decisions as to their future.

Suddenly Carla took a chance and blurted out a question she had been longing to ask for quite a while.

'Peggy, have you seen or heard anything from Paul?'

'What? That's a funny question, but come to think of it, no, I haven't.'

'Neither have I. I did go out with him a couple of times after my birthday do, but he seems to have suddenly disappeared. It's not like him not to even leave a note for me.'

'Well, why don't you ask the welfare officer? He'll know.'

'I never thought of that. Thanks, I will, though I had better wait until this meeting is over.'

The room where the meeting was held was full to bursting. A line of important-looking men were seated up on the platform.

One by one they stood and spoke. A great thank you was due to all the men and women who had been asked to leave their homes and had worked long hours with no let-up. Each speech ran along the same lines until the last gentleman rose to his feet and cleared his throat.

'We have not yet finished with you, ladies and gentlemen.'

This short sentence was met with puzzled silence, and the speaker carried on.

'Of course you all want to get home to be with

73

your families, and this particular factory will be closed down and cleared out within the next week. However, we shall be asking for volunteer machinists to work at our place in Chiswick. No, no more uniforms, not at this point in time, but the government has declared that every serving man who is being demobbed shall be given a decent suit to wear on his return to Civvy Street. Provision has been made in several parts of the country for bales of suitable material to be delivered. Unfortunately, it will not be possible for each man to be measured, but suits have been sold off the peg before now. There will be no charge to any serviceman.'

There was a long pause. No questions were forthcoming and so the speaker continued.

'Any offers to participate in the making of what will be known as "demob suits" will be gratefully received. If any of you have questions, please raise your hand and I will do my best to answer them.'

Peggy had never been backward in coming forward. She stood up and her arm shot up.

'Please, just who would these suits be for? Mainly officers, I presume.'

'Well, young lady, you presume wrongly. Every man being demobbed will be eligible for decent clothing before he leaves the forces.'

'Thank you,' Peggy murmured as she sat down again.

'Every branch will benefit,' the speaker repeated. 'The army, the Royal Navy, the merchant navy and the Royal Air Force. And many others who have

74

proved their loyalty to this country in so many ways without having been in the limelight.'

When everyone had thoroughly understood what they had been told, the meeting was declared closed and there was a general move towards the canteen. Once everyone had a hot drink in front of them, the chattering began.

'What do you reckon, Peggy?' asked Carla. 'Is it something that would be worth our while?'

'Well, for me the best part is working in Chiswick, right on my doorstep once again, and it's not too difficult for you to get there either.' Peggy was quick with her answer.

'True, and who knows whether there is going to be any other paid work about?'

'Yeah, now the boys are coming home, they will be wanting their jobs back, and where will that leave the likes of you and me?'

'For once we have been given a choice, so how about it, Peggy? What say we ask for a couple of weeks off, spend some time with our families and then give this demob-suit making a trial?'

'I'm with you, Carla, we'll give it a go. I expect there will be expert cutters there and all we'll have to do is run up jackets and trousers. It'll be easy as pie after all those fiddly officers' uniforms we've been doing.'

Carla sighed.

'Now what's the matter?' Peggy said.

'I was thinking of the marvellous sewing machines

we shall be leaving behind, here in Southend. You can bet your life we won't see the likes of them again. Wouldn't it be great if sometime in the future we could get our hands on one of them?'

'Be fair, love,' Peggy urged. 'The machines we first used at Chiswick were damn good ones. On the other hand, no one could blame us for comparing those to the ones we've been using here. I wouldn't go so far as to say the difference was like chalk and cheese, but we know it was, don't we?'

'We certainly do. Never mind, we've been told the work won't be so heavy, in which case the Chiswick machines should be perfectly all right.' Carla suddenly sat up straight. 'Peggy, I've just seen the welfare officer go into his office. Will you wait for me if I just pop over and have a word with him?'

'Course I will, I'll get us both another drink. Don't be too long.'

Carla was only gone a few moments before she returned holding a sealed envelope.

'Looks like Paul has left you a letter after all,' Peggy said, smiling broadly.

'Yes, apparently it has been lying there waiting for me for several days. You'd have thought somebody could have brought it to me, wouldn't you?' She took a sip of her tea and then quickly tore open the envelope and began to read:

Dearest Carla, the end of the war may just have brought me some good news. An American surgeon is here in England, he is a friend of my father's and there is a chance that he may be able to be of help to me regarding my ankle. I will keep you posted. Paul.

'Short and sweet,' said Peggy. Tact was never her strong point, but then she had second thoughts. Leaning across the table, she took hold of Carla's hand and said softly, 'I'd lay you twenty to one that Paul will not lose sight of you. He'll be in touch no matter what happens.'

Carla was not exactly over the moon, but she did her best to smile as she tucked the letter into her handbag. Silently she was saying a short prayer. She did so want to meet up with Paul again, and now maybe she was going to be given a chance.

Peggy thought it best not to dwell on the subject. 'What about Elsie and her two little ones? It'll be hard saying goodbye to them.'

'Of course it will be, but we won't lose touch with them, will we?'

'Certainly not. Once we've settled back home, we'll have them up and show them some of London's sights.'

Carla's face changed and she said quietly, 'I hope and pray that Elsie's husband comes home safely to her and the two little ones. I know Elsie has received letters quite regularly, but she has never discussed her man with us, has she?'

'All we can do is wait and see. We certainly won't

lose touch with her, and God knows both of us are going to miss those kids.'

'Right, so what's on the programme for these next few days?' Carla asked, then hastily answered her own question. 'Clearing up, mucking out and getting ourselves back up to the smoke to try and decide what we're going to do for the rest of our lives.'

'Oh, so you've got it all worked out then.'

'Oh Peggy, I don't think we've come out of this war too badly. We've both got a nice little nest egg put away in the Post Office, haven't we?'

'Yeah,' Peggy laughed. 'Only because there's been sod all to buy in the bloody shops.'

'Thanks for everything, Peggy,' Carla said. 'We've come through all our ups and downs together and we certainly shan't lose sight of each other when we are back in London.'

Peggy had to brush away a tear before she could answer, and when she did, she emphasised her words. 'Good friends are hard to find, and if the war hasn't been able to part us, there must be a future for us together somewhere.'

What a week that last week in Southend turned out to be.

Rows of expensive sewing machines fell silent. Cupboards were turned out and shelves wiped clean. Walking to work, the girls were stopped numerous times by local folk wishing them well and assuring them that they would be missed. Both Carla and

Peggy were able to say honestly that they would miss Southend in return.

The morning had arrived. A car was picking Carla and Peggy up to take them to the railway station, and they were both thankful that Elsie had decided that she and the children would say their goodbyes in the house. It would have been heart-rending to take their leave on the platform.

The girls had spent two days touring the shops trying to find something really nice to buy as presents for Elsie, Teddy and Rosie. There was very little choice. They did manage to find a beautiful pale blue twinset which they thought Elsie would like. They had both given up some of their clothing coupons to enable them to buy it, and the shop had gift-wrapped it in a lovely box.

For the children, the choice had been even harder, there were so many empty shelves in the toy shop. However, the owner had said that he did have a delivery of new stock due, and having sold the girls gift vouchers, he took Elsie's name and address and promised to write to her when the stock arrived. That way the children would be able to make their own choice.

To tell the truth, both girls were relieved when it was time to go. Having hugged both the children and finally Elsie herself, they ran down the front path and got into the car. By then they were both quietly sobbing. It had been like saying goodbye to their second family.

Chapter 11

At Fenchurch Street, Carla and Peggy whistled up two taxis. Kisses and numerous hugs, promises of meeting up within days of being home, and the two girls who had lived together for twenty-four hours a day for so long finally parted.

Carla just couldn't relax. She leaned forward to see out of the cab window. My God, she sighed, it was going to take years to replace all the buildings that had been demolished. At least that would provide work for a great number of men, though where the materials would come from was another matter.

These thoughts were banished from her head when finally the cab turned into Tilbury Terrace. Her jaw dropped and her eyes almost popped out of her head. From the small houses on both sides of the street banners were flying: WELCOME HOME CARLA, WE LOVE YOU. What on earth have I done to deserve all this? she was asking herself as the door of the cab was flung open and her aunts were there in full force, surrounded by her cousins, who at first glance seemed to have grown so much it was hard to recognise them.

Good wishes were being called out from all quarters, and Carla was amazed at the welcome. Just as she was about to step down from the cab, the crowd parted and Mr Bristow, who lived opposite, appeared, pushing a wheelchair in which her grandad was sitting. Carla jumped down on to the pavement and almost fell into Grandad's lap. Tears of joy and relief were running down her face as she lowered her head to kiss his cheek. The elderly gentleman was himself very near to tears as he stroked her hair and murmured her name over and over again.

'Can we manage to get us all inside the house?' Daisy was urging everybody.

'Well don't forget tomorrow we're having a street party!' one neighbour called out.

'Yeah, we postponed it on Victory Day,' Mr Bristow explained, 'but now we have a few men that have returned home, and you of course, Carla, so we're going to have a bash.'

Carla wasn't sure if she should be pleased or not. After all, her Uncle Fred was never going to come home, and she wasn't sure what the news was on Sid, Jack and Albert. She needed time to think, but most of all she felt she could murder a cup of tea. Let's hope they've got some fresh milk and they haven't used up all this month's tea ration, she thought.

By four o'clock the next afternoon, the whole street had undergone a transformation. Two long trestle tables had been laid up ready for the tea party. At the bottom of the road three may trees were still standing in the garden of a bombed-out house. Their branches covered with foliage stretched over the broken fence, making a lovely picture – a reminder that it was possible for some things to survive the horrors of the hateful war.

Words could not possibly describe the happiness that both children and adults felt that afternoon. Laughter rang out, and as the smaller kiddies sang a song and were given a prize, even the most hardened adults there could be seen brushing a tear from their eyes.

Lots of the older men were asking whether the country had learnt anything from those years of war. There wasn't a soul present who could answer that question.

'How about you, Carla, have you got your future well and truly planned out?' Mr Bristow asked.

Carla laughed. 'You might not believe me when I tell you that I and many others have been engaged to stay on for a while and complete our war work by making what will be known as "demob suits".'

'What the hell does that mean?' he asked.

'That every member of His Majesty's forces, on being demobbed, will receive a suit free of charge.'

'Bloody 'ell, and are you going to be one of the tailors that make these suits?'

'For the time being, yes. Me and a good few others up and down the country.'

Come evening, Carla sat with her grandad in the parlour, the curtains drawn back and the windows wide open. On a table in front of them stood a pint glass which had been filled with beer for Grandad, and for Carla there was a gin and tonic.

A head appeared at the window and a hearty voice said, 'Here you are, Grandad, we've brought you a tot of good malt whisky.'

Carla couldn't hide her amusement as Grandad struggled to lean forward to take the glass. 'Leave it be, I'll get it,' she called out as she got to her feet and went to the open window.

At twelve o'clock the next day, Peggy turned up on the doorstep.

'Would you like a cup of tea?' Daisy asked.

'Yes, please, I'd love one.'

They all went into the kitchen and settled down at the table.

'Have you learnt much about what's going on yet?' Carla asked Peggy.

'No, not a damn thing that'll make us any wiser. Just that there is to be a meeting the day after tomorrow. My mum said you can come back with me today and stay a couple of nights if you'd like to.' After a pause, Peggy said, 'If we do take up this work, we'll want to know how long it is going on for, won't we?'

'Of course we will, and that's not the only question that needs ironing out. We shall be working in Civvy Street and we need to know how much we are going to get paid.'

'Too true,' Peggy agreed.

The whole household came out into the street to see Peggy climb into her taxi. As it prepared to move off, Carla blew a last kiss. 'I'll see you at the meeting,' she called.

'Jesus wept!' Carla exclaimed as Peggy led her into the warehouse where they had worked before being shipped out to Southend. 'This place has had quite a facelift.'

'That's not all. I've a few more surprises in store for you. First off there is now a very nice restaurant and a rest room, and as well as new toilets, a bathroom has been installed.'

'Who on earth is going to want to take a bath?' Carla queried as she gazed at the new bathroom, in which every luxury modern device had been installed.

'Can't answer that one,' Peggy said, 'but we have three quarters of an hour before the meeting is due to start, so I suggest we take advantage of the facilities and go and get ourselves what should be a decent cup of coffee.'

Carla stood looking in amazement at the newly fitted-out restaurant.

'They certainly haven't let the grass grow under this place, have they? Wasn't this building affected by the air raids?'

'Of course it was, really badly, but miracles can be worked when the spirit is willing. Come on, sit yerself down and I'll fetch the drinks.'

Left on her own, Carla leant her head back and closed her eyes for a moment then blinked.

Everywhere she looked had been refurbished. It just goes to show, she thought, that in this life it's not what you know that counts, but who you know. Like the factory in Southend, these premises were government-owned.

Did it feel good that she and Peggy might be starting work here again? Yes it did, she told herself. When Peggy arrived with the coffees and two very creamy cakes, Carla still had a look of amusement about her.

Placing the tray on the table, Peggy asked, 'What the hell has got into you? What's so funny?'

'I've been counting my blessings, if you must know. You *could* say we're back where we started, but the improvements in this place are unbelievable – can't wait to see the factory itself.' Then she had to stop talking, because her cream cake was demanding all her attention.

'Carla – mind you don't spill that coffee – put the cup down and tell me what's tickling you *this* time?'

'Everything is so perfect.'

'And you find that funny?'

'Not really, but the picture in my mind is of those well-heeled old gentlemen tailors who showed us the ropes when we first came here to work.'

'And? I'll lay you a dollar to a pound they won't put in an appearance this time.'

'How d'you work that out? Think back,' Carla went on. 'On our arrival a lot of the work was officers' uniforms that they were cutting the material for. You don't think they'll be offering their services when it comes to free demob suits for the masses, do you?'

'I have only just realised, Carla Schofield, you are an out-and-out snob, and cynical with it.' Peggy was scolding her but smiling at the same time, and suddenly the pair of them were laughing fit to bust.

Chapter 12

The day had arrived for work at the factory to start once again.

Carla had spent the Sunday with Peggy's family, and now, on Monday morning, they were on their way to the factory. As they walked, they heard hurried footsteps and turned to look behind them. What they saw had them both smiling. Paul Robinson was hurrying towards them.

Drawing level, he put an arm around each of them and pulled them close into a bear hug.

'Don't tell us you are starting work with us again,' Peggy remarked as they walked on.

'No, I'm kind of wishing I was, but I wanted to meet up with you before I go away,' Paul said in a voice that sounded very serious.

Neither of the girls felt they should question him, and so the three of them walked along in silence until Paul stopped dead in his tracks and told them quietly, 'In two days' time I am going to America.' He turned to Carla. 'I owe you an apology, going off and leaving you like that. I am truly sorry and I will explain fully sometime today, as soon as I get the chance.'

They were now within sight of the factory and they quickened their footsteps.

Their arrival was a bit hectic: so many old friends to greet, no one really knowing where they were supposed to go. Finally two well-dressed gentlemen appeared and read out a list of names, instructing those on the list to follow two ladies standing to the left of them.

Carla and Peggy had been at the top of that list, and they both heaved a thankful sigh. 'At least we are still going to be working together,' Peggy murmured.

They all trooped down two corridors, and then a set of double doors was thrown open.

To say that the ten girls were overwhelmed when they saw the sewing machines and their new working surroundings would have been putting it lightly.

On a side table near each machine lay a pile of bales of men's suiting. It looked as if there were three colours: dark brown, navy blue and a dark grey.

A well-dressed gentleman who looked to be in his early sixties rapped his knuckles on a table.

Everyone was so engrossed with taking stock of these new premises that nobody responded. He rapped again, louder this time, and this time he got their attention.

'Ladies, I am Mr Stapleton and I am in charge of this department. Each machine has a memo attached to the front of it that will tell you the size of the suits you will be making. That way, confusion should be avoided. When the first batch of suits are completed, a few men will be coming here to try them on, and if any alterations prove to be necessary, they will be seen to right away.

'We welcome you back to Chiswick and hope you will enjoy your work in these new premises. Meanwhile, it will take some time for the electrics to be switched on and tested, and so you may partake of coffee or tea and even a cake of some kind free of charge for today. The whistle will sound when the machines are ready for you to start work.'

Nobody knew where to look first. Peggy, who had been seated three machines away from Carla, called out, 'I am to be turning out size sixteen suits. What about you?'

'Same as you, sixteen.'

'Not me, I'm to be doing size eighteen,' Mabel Turner said. She was seated on the other side of Carla and they had got on well when they had previously worked together, though Mabel had never been sent to Southend because she had an invalid mother living at home

'Wonder when they are going to turn the electrics on for us to start work,' one young lady at the end of the row called out.

Mabel was looking a little bewildered and Carla asked her what was wrong.

'Well, there seems to be a good supply of cloth and it feels to be of quite a nice quality, but there's no sign of any cutters yet.'

'In that case we might as well head for the canteen, or whatever the place is going to be known as now.' This advice was offered by Peggy and soon followed by everybody on the work floor.

Gasps of wonder and delight came from those who hadn't seen it before as they streamed into the brand-new cafeteria.

'Wonders will never cease!' Peggy voiced the words loudly and a small cheer went up.

Members of staff had been told that for today refreshments would be free of charge. When their forewoman reminded the workers of this, there was a noticeably heartier cheer. The food on offer looked so scrumptious, no one was in any great hurry to make their choices.

Peggy and Carla grabbed a table for two. The coffee was delicious, as before, and the scones had real butter in them – even though rationing was still in place – and the home-made jam was almost as good as Brenda's.

A few minutes later, Peggy spotted Paul standing in the doorway trying to attract Carla's attention.

She nudged her friend: 'Go on, slip away. I'll come and find you if we're needed.'

Carla sensed herself blush, and her heart was pounding. She felt like a sixteen-year-old creeping off to meet her first boyfriend. To her surprise, as she drew near Paul reached out, took her arm gently but firmly and guided her into a secluded alcove below a flight of stairs.

His first kiss was long and lingering. 'Oh my dearest Carla, you will never know how guilty I felt at having to go off without explaining to you what was happening.'

'I forgive you Paul, but only if—' She paused.

Paul murmured, 'Only if what?'

'Only if you hold me tight and kiss me again, please.'

'Carla my darling, you will never have to plead.'

No more words were possible. He had gathered her into his arms and his body was as close to hers as it was possible to get, then slowly but surely his lips were again closing over hers and Carla's eyes were brimming with tears.

'Please, my darling, don't cry. This trip to America will be good for me. My father's surgeon friend is positive that there is a team there that can operate on my ankle.'

'Then I wish you good luck, Paul. I am only sorry we didn't get to know each other better before we left Southend.'

Paul's face became serious before he spoke. 'The

fault was entirely mine. Since meeting you, I have never been more conscious of my ankle, and it made me keep my distance.'

'Oh Paul, we seem to have wasted so much time,' she sighed, then quickly added, 'I don't suppose you have any idea how long you will be away, but will you write to me?'

'I most certainly will. I have made it my business to have your home address, and Peggy's too, because I know you stay with her family sometimes.'

'How about the rest of today?' Carla's voice didn't sound very hopeful.

Paul looked at his watch. 'I hate to say this, but I really have to go. Come outside with me while I wait for a taxi.'

Carla had a lump in her throat that was choking her. She and Paul had met up and it was absolutely wonderful. But in a few minutes they'd be parting again.

All too quickly a cab drew alongside them. As Paul took her in his arms, the cab driver had to look away. Another kiss, another hug and he was leaving her. The door slammed shut and the driver swung the cab around to travel in the opposite direction, and so Carla never even got another glimpse of Paul.

Sighing, she made her way back into the factory and headed for the new washroom. Having washed her hands and face, she used one of the fresh towels to dry herself and then set about tidying up her hair.

'Well?' was Peggy's greeting when she returned to finish her coffee.

'Short and sweet, but I am truly grateful to have at least seen Paul before he goes to America.'

'That's the spirit, girl, and now I've got some news. No work today. Seems some of the leads to the machines are not long enough. So it's back home and we start in earnest tomorrow morning.'

As they left the new premises, they stopped at the corner and stared back at the large building. Carla broke the silence.

'This demob–suit business is only a stopgap for us, Peggy,' she said. 'We mustn't lose sight of that. Once it is over and done with and we have finished doing our duty, we have to start making plans for our own future.'

'Yes, Ma'm.' Peggy gave a mock salute, then, both in stitches, they parted and made their separate ways home.

Three weeks had slipped by, and staff on every level seemed entirely satisfied. Today was to be the climax. The atmosphere on the shop floor was charged with anticipation, but the mood lightened as twelve men of various ages and sizes trooped on to the rostrum. It didn't take long for all the women who had been involved in the making of these suits to breathe a sigh of relief and allow a smile of triumph to come to their faces.

Today's trial was to make sure that the size and

cut of the finished suits were more than adequate. The finishing touches, such as buttons sewn on by hand, were the icing on the cake, and as members of the management committee walked between the men who were acting as models, their words of approval could plainly be heard.

Only two of the models were asked to step out of line; in both cases alterations were needed to the jacket sleeves, which were too long. A volunteer stepped forward, tape measure at the ready, and soon pins were in place to indicate how much shorter the sleeves should be.

Parade now over, a very jovial atmosphere prevailed. The men declared how good the suits were, as well as the various colours and the quality of the material. All expectations had been surpassed. The women too had their say. They all agreed that they had been taken by surprise at just how good the suits looked on the men who had modelled them.

Mr Stapleton stood in the centre of the stage and called for silence.

'First, the management would like to give a vote of thanks to each and every person that has been involved in the making of these suits for our newly demobbed men. Our performance has been repeated the length and breadth of Britain, and it goes to show that as a country we can always be relied on to pull together. We sincerely hope that our lads who are now going to face Civvy Street will be pleased with their suits. Before we break for some refreshment, we shall have two minutes' silence to remember all the men and women who lost their lives whilst fighting to keep this a free country.'

There was complete silence and hardly a dry eye as everyone present remembered with sorrow what the cost of the war had personally been to them.

Chapter 13

Carla thumped hard at her pillows before settling them behind her shoulders. Brenda had brought her a cup of tea before she had taken Joseph to school. She'd told Carla to have a lie-in, but Carla had too many thoughts buzzing around her head. She was twenty-three years old, and where was her life going to lead her now? She had a nice little sum of money in the Post Office, but there was nothing tempting on offer as a way to make a living in an interesting or useful way.

She swung her legs over the side of the bed, grabbed her washbag and went down the five steps to what was known as the bathroom, although the only bath that had ever been there was the tin one that rested against the wall alongside the toilet.

When anyone wanted a bath, the water had to be heated in the gas copper in the scullery, and then carried upstairs in a bucket. It took four or five journeys to fill the bath, by which time the water was lukewarm.

Our way of life can only get better! Carla vowed. She was going to own her own business, and eventually a house with a large kitchen. There would be a deep sink, and above that two taps, one for cold water and one for constant hot. Two more things were to be essentials in this longed-for dream home. One was a comfortable front room with deep armchairs, to be used every day rather than just on high days and at Christmas. And the third compulsory item? A modern bathroom!

An hour later, Carla tiptoed into Grandad's room, where she received a surprise. Brenda was seated on the end of Grandad's bed, and a tray of tea and jam doughnuts was laid out on a side table.

'Proper old sleepyhead, ain't yer?' Grandad teased.

'Look who's talking. Living it up like a lord, you are, by the look of things,' she shot back before putting her arms around his neck and planting a kiss on his forehead.

After their tea and doughnuts, Brenda and Carla tidied the room. The window was wide open, Grandad's armchair and footstool were in place, and very soon the girls had him comfortably seated with a big shawl tucked over his knees. 'There you are, now you can see the world and his wife go by, and it's odds on that some folk will stop and have a chat with you.'

'So what are the pair of you up to?' he asked.

'I've a copper full of washing that needs doing, and today is just fine to get it all out on the line,' Brenda told him.

'Me, I'm going to be footloose and fancy free,' Carla laughed. 'Though there is one thing you might be able to enlighten me about. That big property up there at the end of the road. What did it used to be, and any idea who owns it now?'

'At one time it was owned by a brewery firm, but from what I've heard there's not much of it left to belong to anyone. It certainly took its share of damage from the air raids. Rumour has it that the tenants deserved all they got because they weren't that careful about showing lights; no respect for the blackout. The wardens were always up there shouting, "Put those ruddy lights out!" But there was a time when that house was magnificent and the grounds were truly beautiful. Three gardeners were employed full time, and garden parties were the thing of the day, especially for the Conservative Party.'

'I might have a walk up there. If I do, I'll tell you all about it when I get back.'

'Curiosity killed the cat, you remember that, pet. Don't go climbing about up there, it can't be safe.'

'I shall be very careful, don't you worry.' She leaned over and kissed his forehead again. 'I'll see you later.'

Carla went upstairs. She had no intention of going

to visit a bomb-damaged building in one of her good dresses, and she quickly changed into a pair of black trousers. Grandad hated to see her wearing trousers, but for what she had in mind this morning they would be much more appropriate. She pushed a woolly hat into her handbag, telling herself she might be glad to tuck her long, thick hair up out of the way later on.

She almost rushed out of the house, a look of resolve on her face.

She had thought of climbing the fence at the end of their terrace, but as lovely as that line of may trees looked, they would surely prove to be an obstacle. So instead she walked briskly through the busy streets, and was soon approaching the front of the building.

The large wrought-iron gates had been separated; one was propped up against the wall, the other was lying flat on the ground. She walked on slowly and gingerly, careful of where she was putting her feet, there were so many pot-holes. When what had once been a glorious building came into view, she felt tears sting her eyelids. How could the owners of such a property have just abandoned it? She turned her back and let her eyes roam over the neglected gardens, then, feeling tired and slightly despondent, she allowed herself to sink down and rest on the steps leading up to the front door. She was lost in thought when a male voice brought her back to her surroundings.

She turned her head and looked up. A tall, sturdily built middle-aged man had opened the door. He had dark hair and light brown eyes. His shirt-sleeves were rolled up to the elbows and his bare arms were tanned. He was staring down at Carla, obviously surprised to see her sitting there.

'Yes, miss, is there something I can do for you?' he asked with a smile that immediately put Carla at ease.

'I suppose I had better tell the truth,' she said. 'Curiosity mainly. I find it hard to believe that such a beautiful house has been so neglected.'

'Did you come here by car?'

'No, I only live a stone's throw from here, in a terrace that is bordered by your lovely row of may trees.'

'Did you climb over?' His question was asked abruptly.

'No, but I rather wish I had. It was a long walk and I didn't realise the sun was so hot.'

His face broke into a wide smile that made him look younger. 'Well in that case, the least I can do is ask you in and offer you a cool drink.'

Goodness me, Carla thought. That was far more than she had dared to expect. She scrambled to her feet and looked up at him. 'That is really kind of you and I am not going to refuse.'

'Well, you will have to be very careful. Most of the floorboards are sturdy but occasionally I have come a cropper.'

Inside, Carla was surprised. Layers of dust were to be expected, but the overriding impression was still that this house had indeed been magnificent. It was then that she remembered her manners. Holding out her hand she said, 'My name is Carla Schofield. I was born round here but I have been away for the whole period of the war.'

He took her hand, shaking it firmly as he said, 'Arthur Townsend. There was a time when this was my grandparents' home. Come through to the kitchen. It's the only place that is reasonably clean.'

When much later Carla looked at the alarm clock that stood on a huge dresser and found that it was three o'clock, she shot a glance at Arthur Townsend and they both burst out laughing. He had made two pots of tea and rustled up three packets of biscuits, and they had talked enough to take the hind leg off a donkey.

He now knew that she had been in Southend making uniforms for the forces and was temporarily engaged in making suits for men who were being demobbed. In turn, he had told her that he was a doctor and had been assigned to work with the merchant navy for the duration of the war. He was now at a loose end, in no hurry to make quick decisions about his future.

'So we are agreed,' he said as he took their cups and saucers over to the sink. 'Both of us have had an interesting war and are now resting on our laurels.'

There was no answer to that, so Carla picked up a tea towel and wiped the cups and saucers that Arthur had just washed.

'Let's go for a walk,' Arthur suggested.

'Would you think me very rude if I declined?' Carla said. 'I have enjoyed this afternoon, and although I came uninvited, you have made me feel so welcome. However, if I don't get back soon, my grandad will start to worry about me.'

'Carla, I think you will agree that we have very quickly become friends, and now I am offering you an open invitation to visit this house whenever you wish. I don't come here every day, but four or five times a week, and I usually bring some food with me which you would always be welcome to share. Now, I have my car round the back and it will be my pleasure to run you home.'

'Thank you for the invitation to come again, and I will take you up on that, but there is no need for you to see me home.'

'I did not offer because of a need, but because we have obviously enjoyed each other's company so much I want to extend the pleasure.'

'In that case, kind sir, I would very much like to accept your offer.' Then, with a mischievous grin, she added, 'You will be able to wave to my grandad. When he sees me alight from a motor car, the cat will certainly be amongst the pigeons.'

They were almost home, only a short ride away, when Arthur drew the car to the side of the road and turned the engine off. Turning to face Carla, he began to talk.

'I am nearly twice your age, and I do not want you to think I have any desire to behave badly towards you. It is just that I have hardly any family left alive now, and when you appeared on my doorstep it felt almost as though you'd adopted me, or was it the other way around?'

'I don't really know,' Carla confessed, 'but I feel as if I have known you for ever.'

'Well in that case, will you come up to the house again tomorrow?'

'Yes please,' she said, her intuition telling her that she could safely trust this man.

As Arthur turned the key in the ignition, they were both smiling, and that was how Grandad got his first glimpse of Arthur Townsend when he pulled his car to a halt directly outside the open window.

Carla waved at him and Arthur nodded his head, while Grandad leaned forward, the look on his face a picture.

'Would you like to come in?' Carla asked, but only out of politeness. She felt she would much prefer to be given some time to explain to Grandad just what she had been doing all day, and why a strange man had brought her home in a motor car.

Arthur felt he knew exactly what was passing through Carla's mind and he was in full sympathy with her. Turning to face her, he said, 'I think we have progressed far enough for our first meeting.

You can tell your grandfather that I am an honourable gentleman and that I hope to meet him soon.'

'I'll do that, Mr Townsend,' Carla said, smiling, as he got out of the car, came round to the other side and held the door open for her.

They stood on the pavement for a minute or two until Arthur said, 'I'll look forward to seeing you tomorrow.' Then he turned to face Grandad and smartly saluted him.

Carla waited on the pavement until the car was out of sight. Then, taking a very deep breath, she prepared herself to face the inquisition that was sure to follow.

Chapter 14

Carla was sitting on the steps of the big house just as she had been two months ago when Arthur had first opened the door and invited her in. As she looked around her, listening to the babble of voices and a great deal of laughter, she was having a job believing that so many changes had taken place in such a short period of time.

Resting on her knees was a thick exercise book, and lying beside her were several pencils. She had done her utmost to keep a catalogue of the many different things that had come about since her first meeting with Arthur Townsend. First and foremost, the whole Schofield family had taken to Arthur and had got themselves involved one way or another with the clearing-up of what everyone was now referring to as The Highland House.

Brenda had been the first to accompany Carla on her regular visits and had proved to be most useful. It had been Brenda that had invited Arthur to join the family for Sunday dinner, where he had got to know them all and gained Grandad's approval. Even more so when one weekend he had turned up with a very posh-looking wheelchair as a gift for the old gentleman.

There were plenty of willing hands to carry him out to Arthur's car while the wheelchair was easily stowed in the boot. And for Grandad to be out in the fresh air was as good as any miracle.

Arthur had become part and parcel of the Schofield family, and while he seemed to think that it was he who had benefited the most, the rest of them would have disagreed with that. Not only had he given Grandad a new lease of life, but he had taken Carla's young cousins under his wing, and to watch them all tearing about together was a joy.

The boys thought it was wonderful to be allowed to come to Arthur's big house at weekends with their parents. They could run riot in the grounds, as well as help with such things as picking up rubbish, and Arthur always gave them a couple of pennies each when it was time to go home.

Carla's three uncles, Sid, Jack and Albert, all had their own jobs but had been only too pleased to use some of their free time to take part in the project to restore The Highland House. They each owned a van, which was proving to be a godsend in many ways, especially when there was debris that needed to be carted away. On the other hand they never passed a bomb site without stopping to see what was to be had. If and when work were to start on the big house, it would be a problem to find suitable materials.

Arthur had called in two different firms of surveyors to give advice on the restoration work. He was by no means short of money: his father had invested wisely throughout his lifetime and Arthur had been an only child. However, until more information was forthcoming and the right kind of materials to restore this wonderful old house became available, he had decided that all repairs would have to wait.

Later that afternoon, Arthur drove them all home. Carla unlocked the front door while Brenda and Arthur took the wheelchair from the boot and helped Grandad into it. As she stepped inside, a smile appeared on her face. Lying on the doormat were three airmail letters. Bending quickly, she gathered them together and held them against her face. Then she opened her handbag and thrust them inside. She would read them later, when she was on her own. But now, as she turned back to help manoeuvre the wheelchair over the doorstep, she offered up a prayer of thanks. Paul had not forgotten about her.

★

Dinner was over and the washing-up had been done. Now Carla was alone in her room. 'At last,' she sighed as she withdrew the letters from her bag. One was stamped 'New York'; the other two had a Florida postmark. She looked at the dates and laid them out in order.

The first one had her hugging herself. Paul had actually written *I love you.* The second was medical information about the problem with his ankle. Carla got only halfway through the third before the tears started.

My dearest Carla, so dear to me and yet so far away. Should this operation prove to be successful, please say that you will be my wife and that never again shall we be parted. However did I let all that time pass and never take you into my arms? Never even tell you that I fell in love with you from day one and like the idiot I am let time pass thinking you wouldn't look at someone with such a handicap as I have? Now, confession time over, the outlook is good, promising at least. Please God I shall be dancing with my wife on the day we get married.

Carla wiped her eyes. First thing Monday morning she must go to the post office and buy some airmails. She was going to write one hell of a long letter, never mind how much the postage would be. She had an address now and she would write a little every day and post all the pages on Saturday.

She got up from where she had been sitting on the side of the bed and went to her dressing table. Gazing into her mirror, she smiled dreamily. Paul loved her, and whether or not the operation on his ankle turned out to be a success, she was going to be married to him.

'Oh thank you, God, thank you,' she murmured over and over again.

Life was suddenly full of expectations.

Chapter 15

It was raining, the first wet weekend for ages. Most of the family agreed that it would give them time to catch up on a few jobs indoors that needed doing.

Jack had long been promising to take Alan, his and Edna's only son, to the zoo, and today seemed like a good opportunity.

'Any other of you boys like to join us?' he called out.

The response was almost unanimous. Sid and Mary's two boys, Jack and Thomas, and Albert and Daisy's two, John and David, all volunteered with enthusiasm. That left just Joseph.

'Don't you want to come with us, Joseph?' his Uncle Jack asked kindly, as he put his arm around the boy and drew him close to his side.

Joseph looked to his mother, who blinked away a tear and forced herself to smile. 'Of course you are going, my love, that's what we've got our savings pot for.'

'Thanks, Mum,' he murmured.

Jack got in quickly:'And Uncle Arthur has given me pocket money for each of you, so we're going to have a great time.'

Once Jack and the boys had been waved off, the silence seemed unnatural. Sid and Albert said they had things to do and places to go. Mary, Edna and Daisy had plenty of housework to catch up on, and disappeared upstairs to make a start on it.

'I'll make the four of us a nice pot of tea and then I'm going to attack that ruddy great stack of ironing that's been lying about for days,' Brenda said as she filled the kettle.

'I thought I might take you all for a ride somewhere,' Arthur offered gallantly.

'Thanks for the offer,' Brenda said quietly, 'but I really do mean to attack that pile of ironing, and Grandad will want a nap. You two go off, it will be a nice change to have the place to myself.'

Both Carla and Arthur were well aware that it was at times like this that Brenda missed Fred most, but for now they decided to keep quiet. Carla went upstairs and came down carrying a mackintosh.

Brenda looked amused. 'Why the mac? Are you afraid Arthur might make you walk home?'

Carla smiled. 'You never know, he might park the

car quite a way away from where we're going, and then I'd get soaked with all this rain.'

'As I haven't a clue where we might end up, never mind where I'm going to park when we get there. I suppose Carla is playing it safe, but if we don't stop this chitchat and get going, it will be dark before we get anywhere.' Arthur was trying to sound stern, but both the women just laughed.

'All right, I'm ready.' Carla crossed the room and put her arms around her aunt. 'We won't be back too late,' she whispered.

'Don't worry about me, I shall be fine.'

Whatever Brenda had said, Carla still felt anxious about her. It was clear that she missed Fred and felt very lonely. It had been sad to watch Joseph. He was old enough to know that his mother hadn't got a lot of money coming in each week, and that was why he had held back instead of saying that he would like to go to the zoo. As he grew older, he would come to realise just what a strong, loving family he and his mum were part of. Not one of the brothers or their wives would ever see him or his mother want for anything.

It had stopped raining and the sun was doing its best to break through the clouds. Arthur had been driving for about forty minutes when he turned his head to look at Carla and smiled broadly. 'We are almost there.'

'Really, Arthur, you mean you did have a destination in mind when we set out?'

'Yes, but I wanted today to be a complete surprise for you.'

'You really are a very thoughtful man.'

They were approaching a village, and Carla saw a sign by the side of the road: *Welcome to Stanford-le-Hope.*

As Arthur drove through, Carla was quite astounded. It felt as if they had gone back in time. Not so very far from where she had been born and bred, yet she had never even heard of this place. An old-fashioned village with a French name, so quiet and peaceful.

Arthur had slowed down and the car was barely crawling along as he gave her a running commentary. 'That building over to your left is a small hospital . . . On the corner there is a bank . . . That slightly larger building is a school, run by nuns, and their convent is close by. You will see the few shops and the restaurant when we have lunch.'

There were only three other vehicles in the car park. As Carla stepped out of the car, she was immediately aware that the air she was now breathing was different. 'Funny thing to say,' she told Arthur, 'but this air feels not only clean, but almost sweet.'

'That's because it is. No factories or large industry have ever been allowed to operate from this village. We are going to walk to the far end. There is something I want to show you.'

Walking was a sheer joy. The foliage on the trees and bushes was glistening from the recent rain, and the plants and flowers were a mass of gorgeous colour. Carla thought they had reached the end of the village when Arthur took hold of her arm and directed her down a narrow lane towards two very large brick buildings. He took one look at her face and could not resist smiling.

'Wait until we get inside before you make any comment,' he ordered her.

Curiosity was quickly getting the better of Carla, and as Arthur turned the large key that was already in the lock, she almost pushed by him. She stopped, disappointed.

'Empty,' was all she could mutter.

'Exactly.' Taking hold of Carla, he turned her around until she was facing him. 'How many times have I listened to you saying that you wanted to find suitable premises where you'd be able to set up sewing machines and start your own business?'

'Oh Arthur! You are such a kind and thoughtful man. But what if—'

'No,' he said forcefully. 'No what-ifs.' He paused for a moment. 'The loneliness I knew before you turned up on my doorstep was beyond description. You and your family have given me love and affection, and made me feel I am truly welcome in your home. Now I am in a position to help you.'

A single tear trickled down Carla's face as she did her best to smile. 'There are so many questions I need to put to you before we discuss this matter any further, but I cannot find words enough to say how grateful I am that you have gone to such lengths to help me.'

'Well, how about you walk around this building and see what you think. There is a second one if you think you'd be wanting to expand, and I already have a copy of the details.'

The interior was huge and very clean. Carla walked the full length of the floor and came to a halt in front of a door. Turning the handle, she found herself looking at a small kitchen. Beneath a fair-sized window was a deep sink and a draining board. To the left was a small table on which stood some china, a teapot and a shiny brass kettle.

For a moment Carla was speechless.

'Would I be allowed to work from here? Are the buildings for sale outright or would they be on a lease?'

'Stop it, Carla.' Arthur was grinning. 'Stop and take a deep breath. I think we should go and have some lunch. I have booked us a table, and I know from past experience that this restaurant is very good.'

Carla's mind was whirling. Having her own business! Was it within her grasp? Was she capable of making a success of it? Well, she'd thought about it long enough. If she backed away now, she might never get another chance. But what about the sewing machines? Where the hell would she get them from? And did she have enough money?

Stop it! she told herself. For God's sake get a grip. Go and have lunch with Arthur and just be grateful that he has gone to such lengths to help you. Time enough to worry about the details later.

The restaurant was indeed very good. Arthur made her promise to stop asking questions until they had finished their meal: thick tender steaks served with a fantastic green salad. Then came a gorgeous selection of fresh fruits and a bowl of thick clotted cream. Even the coffee tray was a joy to behold, with its tiny bone-china cups and saucers. The thought uppermost in Carla's mind was how the hell had this establishment survived during the war years?

Because the seats in the garden were still wet from the rain, Arthur suggested they go and sit in the car again. He was well aware that Carla had a lot of questions she wanted answers to, and so he made himself comfortable and gave her the nod to start.

'How did you come to hear about these two buildings being for sale?' was her starting point.

'Quite by chance, really. I was meeting a colleague of mine from Westminster Hospital and we decided to lunch here. It was the day the 'For Sale' notice was being erected on the buildings. I thought at the time that they were situated badly, well out of sight. Then, over a period of time, you talked to me about your ambition and I gave it some thought before I made enquiries. Asking questions costs nothing, and I have learnt a lot.'

'Have you spoken to anyone about what kind of business I would want to carry on?'

'Well, so far I have not approached the owners of the site. However, I have met with the manager of the

116

London agency who has been given sole rights to sell the buildings. His name is Martin Baldwin. Obviously whoever makes an offer stands a far better chance if they buy both buildings and agree to a separate entrance being made to give access without trespassing on any other part of the village.'

'My God! You have done your homework.' Carla was finding it hard to believe what she was hearing.

'I have indeed. I made up my mind not to even mention the subject to you until I had dug deep into all the details. I have met Martin Baldwin on three occasions, and he has fallen over backwards to help with advice. If you feel like another walk, we'll go right the way round until we are able to view the buildings from another approach.'

They walked in silence until they were standing in a position to see both buildings from the back. Each one was completely detached, but they were close enough for Carla to realise that it would be disastrous to purchase just one, not knowing who the tenant might be next door and for what purpose he or she might want to use the property.

When she voiced her opinion to Arthur, he told her affectionately that she had a wise old head on her shoulders.

'Have you noticed that we are facing a main road?' he asked. Carla nodded thoughtfully. 'If matters do come to fruition,' he went on, 'what would you say to making the entrance here, at the back of the build-ings? That would enable the present entrance to be blocked up, and there would be no need for vans or lorries arriving to make deliveries to ever encroach on the village.'

'Arthur, you must have spent hours working all this out. I haven't a clue how much it would cost, but by golly, you make it sound such a good working proposition that I am longing to say I want to go ahead.'

'If you are truly interested, I suggest we set up a meeting with Martin Baldwin, listen to what he has to say, ask any amount of questions and take matters from there.'

'Even if I did manage to purchase such a perfect site,' Carla replied thoughtfully, 'I would still need at least two sewing machines. I'm beginning to think I am aiming too high and wasting your time.'

'Let's go back to the car. I have a proposition to put to you. I want you to listen, make no interruptions, just listen carefully until I am finished. Will you do that?'

'Do I have any option?' Carla asked cheekily.

Walking back to the car, Arthur was deep in thought. He would have no qualms about being a sleeping partner if matters did work out for Carla. During the short time that he had known her, he had come to recognise that where business was concerned, she was a natural.

'I suggest that we go into every detail, with Martin to guide us. I personally would be willing to make a bid on the buildings, and if successful, I would then lease them to you. We would do it all legally, with a clause that gives you the option to buy the two buildings outright from me when the business is up and running. That way you would be able to use your own savings to purchase sewing machines and whatever stock you need.'

It was some minutes before Carla could form a reply, and when she did, her eyes were shining.

'Whatever have I done in this life to warrant having a friend like you?' she murmured.

'Shall we shake on it and make our first priority to seek out a good legal firm before we pay a visit to Martin?'

Carla didn't shake Arthur's hand; instead she leaned towards him and gently wrapped her arms around his neck.

To Arthur's surprise, she was silent on the journey home. He laughed to himself at that thought, and then laughed again. He knew the silence wouldn't last.

Arthur was determined not to let too much time pass by, and come Wednesday, he and Carla were on the train to the West End.

Martin Baldwin had every detail typed out, including the fact that the owner of the properties had agreed to a thousand-pound reduction on the asking price if the purchaser was considering buying both buildings.

Arthur also took Carla to a firm of solicitors,

Fenton and Geering, who were local but also had an office in the West End and had been trustees of his parents' wills.

Within a month, everything was settled, and two days later, Arthur took Brenda and Carla out to dinner. Together he and Carla explained the arrangements, and Brenda was so happy for her niece and wished her every success.

This particular evening was to turn into an exciting one for Brenda too.

When they arrived back home, Carla picked up two airmail letters from Paul and went to her room to read them. Arthur asked Brenda to step out into the back yard, as he wanted to talk to her and he didn't want Grandad to overhear what he had to say.

Feeling a bit baffled, Brenda followed him outside.

'Brenda,' Arthur began, standing directly in front of her, 'a lot of my time lately has been taken up with Carla's affairs, but now that they seem set on the right road, I feel I would like to ask you if you would agree to me taking you out for a meal now and then, or perhaps we could go to the theatre together.'

Brenda could not have formed an answer if you had paid her!

'Please will you think about it?' His voice had a pleading note.

'But why would you want to be bothering with me? Is it because you feel sorry for me?'

'Not at all,' he hastened to assure her. 'Brenda, you are a kind and loving person, a very good mother, but like me you are lonely. It would be no disrespect to your late husband if we became good friends. I have never been married; I was engaged at one time but my fiancée sadly died. Life can be very cruel sometimes. We could always take Joseph with us if that would make you feel better. I happen to think he is a very nice lad.'

'May I have time to think about it, please?'

'Of course, take as much time as you like, and then let me know what you decide. I just thought it would be nice for me to have your company sometimes, and I'm hoping you might feel the same.'

Brenda was utterly bewildered. Oh, how she would like to feel his offer was genuine. She was so fed up with always being the odd one out, even though all the family did their best to include her in whatever was going on. Arthur was such a kind man, but she was still not sure whether he had really asked her to go out with him. Time would tell, she told herself, and with that thought she even managed a smile.

Chapter 16

Carla had come to the conclusion that money spoke all languages.

With Arthur at the helm, there had been no hiccups. Within two months, he and Carla were sitting opposite each other in Fenton and Geering's London office. Several legal papers were spread out and Mr Nichols, a partner in the firm, was indicating just where each of them should sign the agreement.

Now everything was completed, there were hand-shakes all round and Carla was offered good-luck wishes from everyone who had been involved in the transaction.

Arthur was driving Carla, Peggy and Brenda to Stanford-le-Hope.

Carla and Arthur had been visiting the site at least twice a week whilst the building work had been going on, and they had both been there to watch her very own sewing machines being installed. Peggy was over the moon to be asked to be in at the start, albeit on a temporary basis, until they had some idea as to whether orders for their sewing would roll in.

This was Peggy's first sight of the two buildings, and she just could not stand still, flitting here, there and everywhere, her excitement a joy to witness.

'Have you any materials on order?' she asked. 'Are you going to advertise locally? Will we be making new skirts and dresses or will most of the work be alterations?'

'Hold your horses, Peggy, we have to play it by ear as we go along, and hope and pray that the gods are on our side. But for now, come into the second building and see where you and I are going to be living and sleeping for the time being.'

Utterly amazed was the only way to describe the look on Peggy's face as she gazed at the two single beds, two wardrobes and, in the far corner of this vast room, two comfortable armchairs and a small table. The best feature of all was the small secluded bathroom and toilet. This set-up was not ideal for a long period of time, but until the future was more secure, it would do.

Peggy stood still, her hands in her pockets. 'Talk about home from home,' she murmured.

'So may I take it that the new lodgings meet with your approval?'

'Can't wait to move in,' was the satisfied reply.

'This is unbelievable. Talk about us being lucky!' said Carla a week later. She and Peggy had the local paper spread out on the table in front of them.

'Just look at that headline,' Peggy almost screamed. NEW LOOK TAKES FASHION WORLD BY STORM.

After the war had ended, women had gone mad for new clothes. Coats, skirts, dresses were flying off market stalls, and the big stores were coining in the money. The traditional look for women's everyday wear had been knee-length, but postwar fashion dictated that all such garments would now be calf-length, which came as a nasty shock for ladies who had recently purchased new outfits.

Carla lost no time in placing advertisements in several newspapers. Within days, she was inundated with requests to lengthen skirts, coats and dresses.

She and Peggy paid a visit to a local warehouse, coming away with lengths of velvet, corduroy, linen, cotton and lace in various colours. Putting their heads together, they drew diagrams of ways in which they could lengthen every article of clothing that was brought into their workroom. They had no intention of just adding a strip of cloth. If a job was worth doing, it was worth doing well, was their motto. They would measure the customer to make sure they knew just how long they wanted the finished article to be. Then, taking into account that new hems would be needed, a length would be cut from the bottom of the garment, the carefully chosen piece of new material would be sewn into the space and the original piece replaced on the bottom. So far, every attempt at choosing a good coordinating material that harmonised with whatever piece of clothing they were working on had proved successful, though sometimes it took more than one attempt before both of them were satisfied.

Not only did they succeed in lengthening every article that had been brought to them; in some cases they changed the outline of a piece of clothing to bring it up to date with the 'New Look' that was sweeping the country. If a few inches of corduroy velvet were needed to bring the length of a coat into fashion, Peggy and Carla did not leave it there. They would use more of the material to make a collar and cuffs as well. A dress could be brought up to date by the addition of a bolero made from the same material as the lengthening inlet.

'I still cannot bring myself to believe that all this work has just fallen into our laps,' Carla said on more than one occasion.

'Me neither. The whole fashion world has been turned upside down. The big stores wouldn't offer to make alterations; their clientele can afford to buy the New Look. But God knows it has been a blessing to us.'

'You've never said a truer word.' Carla's voice now held a serious note. 'I knew I was taking a terrific chance setting up on my own, and without Arthur backing me all the way, I never would have got started. I'm still finding it hard to believe all this performance about the New Look, but it has worked wonders for you and me. I say a thank-you prayer every night before I go to sleep.'

'Yeah, and it isn't going to stop here,' Peggy declared.

'How can you be so sure?'

'Because when I took this week's advertisements into the newspaper, the editor asked if you were going to start advertising wedding outfits soon.'

Carla's face was a picture. 'Dear God, let's clear this backlog before we start thinking of more ideas.'

'Well he did say that when you're ready, he would write out a few ideas for new adverts for you, and he added that he was thinking of giving you favourable terms.'

'Enough is enough for now,' Carla said. 'Tomorrow is Saturday and I am having the day off. I have three new airmails waiting for me, and if I don't write them and get them into the post, Paul will think I have gone off him.'

'Well, if it's all right by you, I might go home for the weekend. I don't want my family to think I have forgotten all about them.'

'I'm sure they won't. I'll catch up with writing to Paul and do my washing and ironing, and then perhaps next weekend I'll take a trip home myself. For now, though, I'll call a halt for half an hour and go and make us a sandwich and a coffee.'

'Best idea you've had today!' Peggy laughed. 'And see if there is any cake left in the tin while you're about it.'

Chapter 17

Carla was deep in thought as she sat staring into space, letting her coffee go cold. In front of her were her two accounts books, kept well up to date. She and Peggy had been trading for six months and it really was remarkable just how well the business had done. The truth was, the New Look had been a heaven-sent opportunity. Word had spread that she and Peggy had a real flair with a needle, and their prices were always reasonable. The editor of the local paper had been as good as his word, and they had already done two weddings. Both had been simple – the families hadn't a lot of money to spare – but Carla had bent over backwards to give them value for money. That very thought pleased her greatly.

At the moment, she and Peggy were working on their largest order so far. A full bridal outfit, plus one matron of honour, two bridesmaids and one very small pageboy. Thinking of the four-year-old brought a smile to Carla's face. Thomas was the little lad's name, and he wasn't at all sure that he wanted to be dressed up in velvet. He was quite pleased with his suit, because he thought it was very much like the suit that his father was wearing; it was only the velvet waistcoat he was protesting about, but when his dad had promised to wear a similar one, he had half-heartedly agreed.

Yes, Carla told herself as she closed the accounts books, she and Peggy were slowly but surely reaping the fruits of their labours and were more than pleased with their rapidly increasing clientele. Even so, she gave a small sigh as she stood up.

For quite a few months the airmail letters that went to and fro between her and Paul had been very regular. He always wrote so lovingly, though hardly ever touching on what was happening regarding the reason why he had gone to America in the first place. Nor had he yet mentioned a date when he might be coming back to England.

Should she ask a few outright questions? Better not, she told herself. Just keep writing and see what you come up with.

Carla and Peggy were having their mid-morning coffee when the street doorbell rang. Peggy jumped to her feet to answer it, but it was a few minutes before she returned. Carla raised her eyebrows as Peggy came across the big open space with her arm around the shoulders of a very frail-looking elderly lady.

'Carla, this is Mrs Pearson. We're doing the outfits for her granddaughter's wedding, and Mrs Pearson would like to know what we can do for her.'

'Would you like a cup of tea?' Carla suggested as she helped the elderly lady with her coat, which she couldn't help but notice was in a pretty shabby state.

'Oh no, thank you for asking, but I have just had coffee in the restaurant and I have booked to go back there for my lunch. It is a long walk from the village and I thought I might as well make it a full day out.'

Well she can't be that hard up, Carla thought. You couldn't always go by first appearances.

'Would you like to tell us what you have in mind?' Peggy had gone straight to the point.

There was a look of concern on Mrs Pearson's face, but no answer was forthcoming.

'Have you a favourite dress or maybe a two-piece suit that you might like us to put a few touches to, kind of bring it up to date?' Carla asked.

'Oh no, my dears. I have heard so much about the two of you and what you are doing for other folk in the bridal party.' The old lady paused, took a deep breath and then boldly declared, 'I want something brand new and different to what anyone else will be wearing.'

'Mrs Pearson, have you spoken to the mother of the bride? That has to be your daughter, am I right?' Carla had spoken quietly.

'Yes, I have, but she just said she hasn't any spare time, she has more than enough to do with all the arrangements and I should please myself.'

'Have you any other children, or just the one daughter?' Peggy gently enquired.

'Oh no, I have another daughter, Joyce. She and her husband are coming this weekend to spend a few days with me.'

'Well there's your answer,' Carla said, beaming. 'While she is with you, why don't you get your Joyce to bring you along here, and between us I'm sure we'll be able to sort out an outfit for you that would be fit for the Queen.'

'How kind you have both been. I shall certainly do as you suggest.' Mrs Pearson stood up and began to pull her gloves on.

'You enjoy your lunch,' Carla called out as she watched Peggy guide the old lady to the front door.

Minutes later the two girls stood facing each other. 'Let's hope her other daughter has more time for that dear old soul than the bride's mother apparently has,' Carla said sadly.

'Makes me realise how lucky we both are,' Peggy replied, her voice sounding very solemn.

131

'Too true it does. Can you imagine any member or your family or mine treating an elderly relation like that? Let's hope this Joyce has a bigger heart where her mother is concerned.'

'Are we going to sit here and while away the rest of the day, or are we going to make a start on some work?' Peggy was raring to go.

'Before we make a move, I have something to tell you, and also a suggestion to make.'

'If it's juicy gossip, then I'm all ears. Let's hear it.'

'Last weekend, while you were away, Arthur called in here.'

'So what? He often comes, doesn't he?'

'Yes, but this time he had a lady with him.'

'Did he now? Who was she? Did you know her?'

'We both of us know her well. It was Brenda, and if you want to know was I pleased, then yes I was. Over the moon, to be honest. Brenda's been so lonely since she lost Fred, and Arthur has been on his own for ages. Nothing might come of it, but for now they seem really happy to be together.'

'Well good luck to them, I say. That's the gossip delivered. Now what is this suggestion all about?'

'Next weekend I'd like you to come home with me, just for a couple of nights.'

'Oh Carla, you know I'd love that. Really I would.'

'That's settled, then. Now, if we are both going to take time off at the end of the week, we'd better get stuck in and see just how many orders we can complete between the pair of us.'

'That's fine by me.'

'Right, well let's get these cups and saucers out of the way and our machines humming.'

Chapter 18

It had been a great week for Peggy and Carla. There wasn't one order promised for the weekend that they had failed to deliver.

They had insisted that each and every customer who came to collect their garments should try them on. Cries of delight rang out as the customers sang their praises. Most declared that they preferred their skirts and dresses that had been altered to the new items available in the shops.

That Friday, there were several moments when both girls sent up a prayer of thanks to whoever had brought the New Look into being.

And now they were both going to the East End to enjoy a family reunion. Carla's only sadness was the absence of her mother. She had been too young to die, and to this day Carla still missed her so much. 'Oh Mum,' she whispered softly, 'how I wish you were here to share in all the good luck that has been coming my way.'

At that moment she heard the front door open and Arthur's loud voice calling out, 'Any coffee going?'

With big strides he covered the space between them and was soon hugging and kissing each girl in turn.

'You must have been up and about early this morning,' Peggy said with a wide grin.

'I haven't come from home; I've been in the West End, winding up some of my parents' affairs that were still outstanding. Couldn't almost pass your front door without dropping in, could I?'

'If you had and we had got to know about it, you would have been in trouble, and we would have found out, because both of us are going home for the weekend.'

'In that case, why don't you come back with me today?'

'Because we're working girls and we just can't drop everything and go. We'll catch an early train tomorrow morning,' Carla was quick to tell him.

'No you won't, I'm not having that. Say what time you will be ready to leave and I shall be here to pick you both up.'

'Oh Arthur, you are a real darling,' Peggy said.

'Well if I'm that good to the pair of you, why hasn't someone offered to make me a cup of coffee?'

Peggy was already on her way to the kitchen; she half turned and called over her shoulder, 'I'll have it ready in two minutes.'

Carla grabbed the chance of being alone with Arthur to say, 'I really was pleased when you turned up here with Brenda. No matter what the outcome may prove to be, I think even friendship is a God-given gift, and I also know how cruel loneliness can be. You and Brenda are both very nice people, and I wish you both all the very best.'

'Thanks, Carla, your good wishes mean a helluva lot. It was so obvious to me that Brenda was always the odd one out, often left in the house on her own. She seems to do so much for others, especially your grandad.'

'How do you feel about Joseph?' Carla hesitantly asked.

'I think he is a really nice young lad, but Brenda and I have agreed to play matters down for the moment. We are both pleased to have the friendship, but slowly does it for the time being.'

'Very sensible, and once again I do wish you both all the luck in the world.'

Arthur's reply to that was to open his arms, wrap them around Carla and hug her close.

'I am standing behind you with this scalding cup of coffee,' Peggy warned. 'I couldn't help overhearing and I'd like to add my good wishes to Carla's.'

Arthur released his hold on Carla and turned to Peggy. Taking the cup of coffee she was holding and placing it on the nearest table, he wrapped his arms around her in turn. 'It feels good to know that Brenda and I have good wishes from both of you. Early days yet, and a whole lot will rest on what attitude Joseph takes. Neither of us would do anything that would hurt that young lad. Losing his father has been enough pain to last him a lifetime.'

'How about my uncles, what kind of reaction have you had from them?' Now that this conversation had got under way, Carla thought it was good to ask questions, get it all out into the open and hope the outcome would be a happy one for everyone.

'So far, so good. They've all offered to buy me a pint when we next meet up in the pub; none of them raised any objections,' Arthur assured her.

'Well drink your coffee and get on your way, because we have quite a few loose ends to clear up if we are coming home tomorrow morning.' Carla was being bossy now.

Arthur sat down and began to sip his hot coffee. 'What time would you two dear young ladies like me to pick you up?'

'As early as you like,' Peggy said.

Carla grinned. 'I agree. You state a time and we'll be on the doorstep with our bags all packed.'

'Oh, so I travel all the way here, and no offer of a hot drink, just a quick turnaround!'

Peggy had a tea cloth in her hand and she flicked it across Arthur's shoulders.

'On your way, Arthur, you are costing us money.

We can't afford to be idle when there is so much work awaiting our attention.'

'OK, I've got the message. I'll see you both bright and early tomorrow.'

The two girls stood out in the open air watching Arthur drive away until the car was out of sight. As they went back inside, prepared to start work again, Carla said, 'Peggy, don't you think the pair of us have a great deal to thank God for?'

'I do indeed. I honestly think somebody must be on our side, because we have both been so very fortunate.'

'Well, let's pray that it lasts. Now it's time we got our machines humming.'

As she watched Peggy's long fingers guiding the material beneath the needle, Carla sighed happily. It seemed almost unbelievable that the two of them got on so well, able to work together without arguments or even differences of opinion. We even share each other's families, she thought with a smile. She was so looking forward to the coming weekend. She hoped nobody had told Grandad that she was coming home; she did so want to give him a lovely surprise.

The weather was promising to be really warm as the two girls opened their front door and stood their cases outside ready for when Arthur arrived.

'We're like a couple of kids going on a school trip,' Peggy giggled as they heard Arthur's car approaching.

Despite their desire to be off straight away, they not only allowed Arthur to come in and wash his hands, they also presented him with refreshments. For Carla now came out of the kitchen carrying a tray holding three steaming cups of coffee and a plate of assorted biscuits. It was a happy trio of good friends who sat in the sunshine contemplating the coming weekend.

'Time to make a move,' decided Arthur eventually. He began to load the cases into the boot of his car, while the two girls checked and rechecked that everything inside the building was safe before finally locking the big front doors. They climbed into the back, and Arthur settled himself in the driver's seat.

'Well here's to a cracking good weekend!' he said.

'I'll second that,' two voices chorused as the car moved off.

It was a lovely easy ride, not much traffic on the roads until they neared the Port of London, just east of London Bridge.

'Not much changes here,' Carla observed quietly, thinking how dirty everywhere looked, but quickly banished all such thoughts from her mind. This was the real London, where she had been born and brought up, and she had better not let her wonderful family think that she had become too big for her boots!

At last Arthur brought the car to a standstill outside the Schofields' terrace. To Carla's joy, every member of her family was standing outside waiting to welcome her home. Her grandad was in his wheelchair by the kerb.

'Grandad!' Carla cried as she got out of the car. She threw her arms around his neck and kissed him. A single tear was trickling down his withered cheek, and she had to swallow hard to get rid of the lump in her throat. 'Oh Grandad, it is so good to see you.'

It was time to get everybody inside. Jack and Edna's house was the biggest, so that was where they were all going to eat.

The table looked inviting, covered with plates and dishes of tempting food. By now most of the men, Arthur included, had a glass of beer in their hands, while the women bustled about making tea and coffee. Mary had made herself responsible for the six boys, who were all growing so fast it was a job to keep up with them.

It took some time, but eventually everybody had been fed and watered, and now the men were bringing the girls' suitcases along to Brenda's house. Jack was pushing Grandad in his wheelchair.

'Need some help, Jack?' Arthur had caught up with them.

'Yes please, mate, just t'get the wheelchair over the front doorstep.'

'No sooner said than done,' Arthur grinned.

Carla breathed a sigh of relief once Grandad was back in the house and comfortably settled.

'You both get off,' she said. 'I'm going to stay with Grandad for a while.'

Jack and Arthur were reluctant to leave the old gentleman; transporting him, then getting him in and out of a different house had been very tiring for him. But Carla insisted. 'Go on,' she said. 'Go back and check that Peggy is all right with all those boys racing round. If I need anything, I only have to call out to Brenda.'

'Well if you're sure . . .' Jack looked at Arthur. 'We won't be far away.'

Closing the door behind the two men, Carla took a small chair and placed it beside Grandad's bed.

'Bless you, my love,' Grandad murmured as he laid a hand against Carla's cheek. She took hold of his other hand and pressed it to her lips.

'Close your eyes and get some sleep, Grandad. I promise I will still be here when you wake up.'

The gentle smile he gave her before he closed his eyes would live in her memory for the rest of her life.

It was late in the afternoon when Brenda quietly opened the door and peeped in to see how Carla was doing with Grandad.

'Looks like you've both fallen asleep,' she whispered, but getting no answer, she walked towards the bed.

The sight of the elderly man and his young granddaughter holding hands while they slept was so peaceful it brought a lump to Brenda's throat. She bent low over Carla and was about to touch her when realisation hit her. She took a step backwards, then lifted her apron and threw it upwards to cover her face. A sob caught in her throat, almost choking her.

Brenda made it to the bathroom, where she knelt down, lowering her head over the lavatory pan, and heaved her heart up. She stayed there for a long while, until she heard Arthur's voice downstairs.

She managed to call out, 'I'm in the bathroom.' But her voice sounded strange even to herself.

In no time at all Arthur was behind her. He took a face flannel from above the washbasin and held it under the tap, then wrung it out and gently wiped her face.

For a long moment silence hung between them, then he opened his arms wide and gathered Brenda's trembling body close to his own. There was no need for words. Brenda gave a long shudder, which made Arthur tighten his hold on her. 'It's Grandad, isn't it?' he asked softly.

Brenda lifted her head and with difficulty said, 'He and Carla are both dead.'

Poor Arthur! He had not been expecting this, and he could barely find the words to answer her. He felt faint himself.

Brenda was a level-headed person, not given to making rash statements. Whatever had happened, she was in a state of shock, but surely she had got this wrong! He began to pray, something he wasn't used to, but like a drowning man he was clutching at straws.

Jack was leaning against the sink smoking a cigarette when Arthur came into the kitchen. One look at Arthur's face, and he needed no telling that something was terribly wrong.

'Jack, will you come upstairs and help me to bring Brenda down, please. She's had a nasty shock.'

'She's not the only one, by the look on your face. Hadn't you better tell me what's happened?'

'You're right, Jack. On second thoughts, I think you and I should go into the front room and see for ourselves. According to Brenda, both Grandad and Carla are dead.'

The colour drained from Jack's face. 'Christ almighty! You've got to be bloody joking!'

'There's only one way to find out. Come on,' Arthur urged as he grabbed Jack's arm.

The curtains were still pulled back and a beam of sunshine had fallen across Carla's face. She certainly looked peaceful, but Arthur noticed at once that a pulse was vibrating steadily at the base of her neck. He pointed this out to Jack, at the same time signalling for his friend to follow him round to the head of the bed.

Neither of them needed any telling. It was obvious that Grandad was dead. To make sure, Arthur leaned across and felt for a pulse, before shaking his head in Jack's direction.

The two men straightened up and stood gazing at Carla, who still had not stirred. By unspoken agreement, they moved to stand on either side of her, gently slid their arms beneath her body and lifted her up and away from the bed. Carrying her out of the room, they sat her down in the kitchen, making sure she was fully awake before they made for the stairs to fetch Brenda.

Poor Brenda was still shaking as they brought her downstairs and settled her on a kitchen chair. Arthur held her hands and began to massage them, talking all the while in a soft, soothing tone.

'Brenda my love, you were right, Grandad has died, passed away peacefully in his sleep. Carla too was in a deep sleep when you found her, and it was natural that you thought the worst, but look, she is with us now, sitting on the other side of the room.'

Brenda lifted her head, and seeing Carla there, she prayed aloud: 'Oh dear God, thank you.'

Jack brought a glass into which he had poured a little whisky. Bending down, he took hold of Brenda's hand and wrapped her fingers around the stem of the glass. 'Brenda, I want you to sip this slowly. We've given the same to Carla. God knows you both need it. That was one hell of a shock for the pair of you, and it hasn't done Arthur or myself much good either.'

Brenda ignored his instructions and tossed her head backwards, letting the whisky run straight down her throat. Then she got to her feet and made her way unsteadily across the kitchen. She knelt down in front of Carla, taking hold of one of her hands and clutching it tightly between her own.

'Carla, can you imagine what Grandad is saying right now?'

She got no reply. Carla didn't even raise her head.

Brenda gently placed an arm around her niece's shoulders and drew her close.

'Well, I shall tell you. He is saying thank you, Lord Jesus, for letting me have my one and only granddaughter with me at the end. My Carla held my hand all the way through the valley of death, and she never let go until the angels opened the golden gates for me.'

'Oh Brenda!'

Both women were sobbing now. And neither Jack nor Arthur was entirely dry-eyed as they drank the remains of their whisky.

Chapter 19

No one in the family could have anticipated how this weekend would turn out.

There had been so much to do, and whichever way they turned, they seemed to be blocked in by legalities. The family doctor had been called, and after giving Carla and Brenda his attention, he had turned his efforts to getting Grandad's body removed from the house as quickly as possible, though before that could happen, the police had to be informed.

Now, the silence in the house was almost unbearable. The door to the front room was closed; nobody wanted to go in there. Between them, the women had rustled up some food, but nobody had felt like eating much.

The silence was broken when they heard the front

door open. Albert and Sid were back from the under-taker's. The firm they had chosen was a well-known and respected one that had certainly fallen over backwards to be helpful. Grandad would be laid out so that visitors could pay their respects, and the funeral would take place in three weeks' time. Albert and Sid explained that the delay was due to legal requirements regarding the family's burial plot.

By now all the adults were gathered and were in complete agreement that Albert and Sid had done their best. They all prayed that everything would fall neatly into place and that Grandad would get the loving send-off he so richly deserved.

Later that night, as Carla and Peggy made their way upstairs to bed, they were both pondering on what they would do during the three weeks before the funeral. On the top step they found Brenda and Arthur sitting side by side, both deep in thought.

'Arthur, we need your advice, please,' Carla said. 'We cannot just leave our business for three weeks; if nothing else, we have a wedding a week from today. Please tell us what you think we should do.'

'Carla, my darling, I am quite sure that everyone will agree it will be for the best if I take the pair of you home in the morning. You can get on with making your living, and you may rest assured that every single detail regarding your dear Grandad's funeral will be attended to with loving care. Will you trust me to help in any way that I can?'

Carla couldn't form an answer; her eyes were

brimming with tears. She took Arthur's hand and held it tightly.

'Bless you, Arthur. I do seem to be imposing on you a great deal. Two things I want to do, and then yes, I will go back to work until the funeral.'

'Name them and I'll help if I can.'

'I want to go and kiss Grandad goodbye, and then I will find a decent florist and place an order.'

'Far be it from me to interfere,' said Peggy, 'but we have a wonderful florist in the village. You could go there, discuss what you would like as a memorial for your grandad and they would make it fresh for us to bring on the day.'

'Good idea,' Brenda said. 'And Carla, I will come with you to see Grandad before you leave.'

'Thanks, Brenda. I am sorry I gave you such a shock. I am also very grateful to you for explaining that Grandad's passing was so peaceful.'

'Well I think it's time that I took myself off home,' Arthur said. 'The sooner you are all tucked up in bed, the better.'

It hardly seemed possible that it was only yesterday that so much had happened. Carla had somehow managed to get a good night's sleep, and Brenda would be going with her to the chapel of rest to see Grandad.

Breakfast had been hectic, friends and neighbours in and out all the time, but finally Brenda and Carla were walking slowly past the dockyards and soon they had reached the undertaker's.

The two men who met them in the front office were immaculately dressed. They suggested that the ladies should go in one at a time.

'Give me your handbag and you go in first,' Brenda whispered to Carla.

The taller of the two men ushered Carla down a long corridor. When he drew to a halt, he opened a door and nodded for her to enter.

Pointing to a red light on the wall by the door, he said, 'Just press that light if you need anything or when you are ready to leave. I shall only be a short distance away.'

When he had left, closing the door quietly behind him, Carla looked around the room. It was a delight to behold. There was a velvet-covered settee and two armchairs placed one each side of an electric fire. On a side table, a truly beautiful glass vase held a floral arrangement. Grandad was lying on a bed, fully dressed and looking so peaceful. A chair had been placed at the side of the bed, and Carla sat down thankfully. Reaching out, she lifted one of his hands and held it against her cheek.

'Wearing your best suit, I see, Grandad, and your shoes have been well polished.' Carla spoke softly. She leaned across to kiss that dear face. 'Don't go too far away, please, Grandad, and don't forget to tell my mum how much I love and miss her. You two look after each other.'

It was all too much. She clutched his hand and again held it close to her cheek for a full minute before laying his arm down by his side. Then, taking her handkerchief from her pocket, she wiped away her tears before leaning over for one final kiss.

On the way home, both women were actually smiling. 'Didn't he look peaceful?' Brenda said.

'Yes, he certainly did, and I am so glad that we visited him. The way he looked today is the way I want to remember him.'

Daisy had cut some sandwiches and laid out the cups and saucers. Every member of the family had come in to hear how the two women had got on at the undertaker's, and they were all reassured by what Carla and Brenda had to tell them.

Arthur broke the gathering up by turning to Carla and Peggy and saying, 'Well, you two workers, I have brought your cases downstairs and they are in the boot of my car, so as soon as you are ready, we can get on the road.'

The goodbyes were sad and quiet, and on the journey both girls were still very subdued. When they got home they bustled about, making eggs on toast and coffee, and finally Arthur said it was time he was on his way.

Peggy and Carla stood waving until the car was out of sight, then both heaved a great sigh. Peggy put an arm round Carla. 'I suppose we should count our blessings. At least you were there with your grandad, and it was such a peaceful end to his life.'

'Yes, I will keep reminding myself of that.'

'Shall we unpack our cases straight away?'

'Yes, I want to hang my clothes up, and then I'm going to have a long soak in the bath.'

'Great idea, I'll follow you, then we'll both be ready to make an early start in the morning.'

Chapter 20

The following morning, Peggy and Carla had their breakfast, washed up, made their beds and were at their sewing machines by eight o'clock. Their full attention was on the wedding that was taking place on Saturday. Carla was putting the finishing touches to the bridesmaids' dresses, and she was well pleased with the result. She was just laying one of the dresses out on the ironing board when the front doorbell rang. 'It's all right, I'll get it,' she called to Peggy.

As she turned the key in the lock and held the door open wide, she was pleased to see Mrs Pearson standing there. Beside her was a very smartly dressed woman, who quickly said, 'I am Joyce Underwood. I understand that you have promised to help my mother with her outfit for my niece's wedding.'

'Please come in. My partner and I did make your mother a promise, and we will do the best we can to fulfil that promise.'

Carla called to Peggy to come and join them. They shook hands and Peggy said, 'I see you have a bag with you. Is it something you think maybe we can trim up?'

Joyce Underwood looked uncomfortable. 'I have done my best to persuade my mother to buy a new outfit for this wedding, but she is standing firm. She has told me what you suggested and I have been through her wardrobe. I think I may have found something decent, but I won't be offended if you think otherwise.'

'Let's have a look, shall we?'

Mrs Pearson's daughter was now opening up the bag she had brought, to reveal a navy-blue two-piece. She passed one half to Peggy and the other half to Carla. The girls held the garments up to the light.

'The material is really good quality' – Carla was speaking more to herself – 'and the skirt seems quite long enough even to qualify for the New Look. So it is only the jacket that needs a facelift. Right, let's concentrate on that. I say we replace these old buttons, for a start.'

Peggy's turn. 'We still have some of that pure linen,' she murmured to Carla. 'Collar and cuffs, what do you think?'

Joyce Underwood now delved into the bag and brought out a very fashionable trilby-shaped hat.

Carla took it from her. It was made of a gorgeous soft, shiny felt, and the label inside said 'Harrods'.

'This would be great for your mother to wear in church, and we could make a new hatband using the same linen we'd trim the jacket with.'

'What do you think, Mother? Are you happy with what these two young ladies are offering to do for you?'

'Very much so. Do you know, Joyce, your father bought me that hat before you were born. I wore it when he took me to see the Derby at Epsom racecourse.'

Mrs Pearson seemed entirely happy, and her daughter very relieved as she asked, 'Will you girls be at the wedding on Saturday?'

'No, though we will be at the rehearsal on Friday. We need to see that all the wedding outfits are fitted and worn properly.'

It was Peggy who saw the two women out. As she rejoined Carla, she said, 'I suppose that most elderly folk are living on their memories.'

'Well if that is true, then you and I had better start storing a few good ones up.'

'Chance would be a bloody fine thing, don't you agree?' Peggy said, chuckling.

'Yes, I do. We'll get our order book clear and then we'll maybe get an opportunity to live it up a bit.'

'Promises, promises. For now it's back to the grindstone.'

'Oh Peggy, don't sound so hard done by. One of

our travelling salesmen told me that his firm is starting up a couple of factories in the Channel Islands – you know, Jersey and Guernsey. It might be on the cards that we'll get invited there for free if they think they stand a chance of obtaining orders for material from us in the future.'

'Yeah, and meanwhile let's get this wedding over and done with.'

On Wednesday morning, Mrs Pearson arrived to try on her refurbished navy-blue two-piece. There was a chorus of approval as she did a twirl.

'Mother, these young ladies have certainly done you proud, and I am going to buy you a new handbag and a decent pair of navy-blue shoes.'

'Oh, thank you, Joyce,' Mrs Pearson murmured.

When they had seen mother and daughter off the premises, Carla turned to Peggy. 'You do realise that come Friday, we have to go through all the fittings?'

'Yes, I'm really looking forward to seeing the bridesmaids' dresses on the twins. I have a funny feeling that the bride's mother will be there, even though we haven't made her outfit.'

'Well, we shall be ready for her. Neither of us has had a moment's worry over the bridal gown, Elaine has been a joy to work with and we won't hold her responsible if her mother tries to interfere.'

The busy week was almost over. Carla kept telling herself not to think about Grandad but to pay full attention to this dress rehearsal. A lot was resting on their first full wedding assignment.

The decision to attend to young Thomas first was unanimous. He really was a charming little boy, and when he was behaving well, one couldn't help but love him to bits.

So far, so good. The one thing that the girls had anticipated Thomas would baulk at was his shoes. The girls were wrong.

As his father helped him to put them on, he said, 'Golly, I wish *I* could have been given a pair of shoes that had silver buckles on them.'

'Daddy, they are special shoes because I am the only pageboy.' Thomas was quick with this information.

'Oh, I see, special shoes for a special boy,' his father responded.

Thomas looked a picture: his neat grey two-piece suit, pure white shirt, and the splendid blue velvet waistcoat.

The bridesmaids' dresses had been a joy to make. They were ankle-length and long-sleeved, the material an expensive silk the colour of a ripe peach. There was a plaited belt made of strips of the material and shreds of silver, and a headband to match to hold the little girls' long fair hair in place. On the day of the wedding they were each to carry a basket of rose petals that they would scatter as they walked down the aisle behind the bride.

Both Carla and Peggy had their fingers crossed

behind their backs as the bride came forward to try her dress on.

Time once again to thank God. The dress slid on as if it was a second skin. The imported shot silk shimmered. As Peggy and Carla fastened the buttons that ran from the neck down to just below the waist-line, they were both holding their breath. The same tiny silver buttons also ran from the wrists to the elbows, while the neckline was a masterpiece, cut into a heart shape and edged with a pure silver plaited band, which also matched the band that would lie across the bride's forehead to keep her veil in place.

Peggy and Carla smiled at each other, silently congratulating one another on a job well done.

On Saturday morning, Peggy and Carla were at the home of the bride-to-be, just to give her last-minute reassurance that she really did look regal. The minute the convoy of cars had left for the church, the two girls could relax.

'Well, given that that was our first ever wedding, I don't think we did too badly at all,' said Carla.

'I couldn't agree more,' Peggy said, and her tone of voice was very serious as she added, 'Please may we go home now? I don't know about you, Carla, but I could eat a damn good fry-up for my breakfast.'

'You have just hit on a very good idea, but we won't muck about cooking, we shall go to our favourite restaurant and be waited on,' Carla declared.

By midday, the pair of them were well fed and watered. Both were looking forward to seeing a copy of this week's local paper. The editor had been given instructions by the bride's mother as to what photographs she wanted to appear. However, he'd been impressed by Peggy and Carla, and he was going to make sure that these two young ladies received a lot of publicity for their part in this wedding.

Chapter 21

The following days really dragged. The girls kept themselves busy, but Carla especially could not concentrate. The morning she heard Arthur's car draw up outside, her spirits rose.

His greeting was solemn and he soon came to the point.

'I think I should stay here tonight and take you back to the family tomorrow.'

'Why?' The same exclamation came from both Peggy and Carla.

'Because the funeral is only days away now, and Carla, so much has been left to your aunts to cope with. I think you could make a difference by just being there.'

'You think I have neglected my duties?'

'I wouldn't dare suggest such a thing. Obviously you had to carry on with the wedding that you had contracted for, but for you to stay here now and work while others make the decisions regarding your grandad's funeral does not sit well with everyone.'

'What about my uncles? Haven't they been pulling their weight?'

'Each and every one of them has more than pulled their weight, but they have their own jobs too. There are so many things that have yet to be decided; finances, for one. No one seems to know whether your grandad had any money or insurance policies. Tell me it's nothing to do with me and I will back off. But on the other hand, I am more than willing to help if your uncles would care to seek my advice.'

'Oh Arthur, I shouldn't just have walked away. I am so sorry that you have been drawn into our family problems. Will you answer me one question: has anyone found solicitor's papers or a will?'

'That's exactly why you should be there. You are able to ask those sorts of questions, whereas if I interfere, I could be told to mind my own business. Do you understand what I am saying?'

Carla nodded. What Arthur was saying was the truth. She had thought only of the wedding she had been working on, and had left her aunts to sort out Grandad's affairs. What could she do to make amends?

'It won't take me long to pack a case,' she said, 'and if it is all right by you, Arthur, I shall come back with you today.' She turned to Peggy. 'What would you like to do?'

'I would like you to come into our bedroom for a few minutes, please,' Peggy said.

Once the two friends were alone, the tears came to both of them.

'Have we been utterly selfish?' Peggy sobbed the words out.

'If we have, then it is my fault. What would you like to do, Peggy? I don't have any choice, but you can stay here or go home to your own family.'

'Please, Carla, don't cast me off. We are such good friends and I'd like it to stay that way. Are you thinking that maybe your family will not want me around this time?'

'Of course they will. There will be no bad feelings, and if you want to come back with me now and stay for the funeral as we had already arranged, then that is fine by me. We can't undo what is done, but I will do my best to see that things are worked out peacefully.'

After the three of them had had a cup of tea, it was decided that Arthur would stay overnight, giving the girls time to pack their cases with suitable clothes for the funeral, and they would set off early in the morning.

They were all up, washed and dressed by six thirty. After a scrappy meal of tea and toast, the cases were loaded into the boot of Arthur's car, and by eight o'clock they were on their way.

On their arrival, the four aunts hugged and kissed Carla, showing no animosity whatsoever, a fact that she was truly grateful for. Peggy too received a warm welcome. The men were at work and the boys all at school. Edna had been to the baker's and bought fruit scones, which she had warmed in the oven. Served with butter and cups of tea, they went some way to making everyone feel a little better.

No one was the least bit surprised when Arthur made his excuses and left to go home.

Edna was washing up and Peggy and Daisy were drying when Carla very quietly said, 'Thanks for the welcome, Edna. I'm going along to Brenda's now and will catch up with you all later.'

'Do you want me to come with you?' Peggy asked.

'Not for the moment. There is something I want to do on my own.'

'All right, but if you do need any help, just call out.'

'I will. Thanks again, girls. If things go according to plan, I shouldn't be very long.'

Mary, Brenda, Edna, Daisy and Peggy looked curiously at each other, but none of them was prepared to question Carla as to what her intentions might be.

Back in the house in which she had been born, Carla went straight through the kitchen and into the scullery. She took her coat off and, moving a small vase of fresh flowers, laid it on the table. Brenda kept this place nice, though it must be an uphill job; these old houses had never recovered from the bombings during the war.

Rolling up her sleeves, she kicked her shoes off and knelt down facing the yellowish stone sink. Ducking her head, she leaned forward, but her forehead was touching the heavy lead pipes that ran beneath the sink and her long hair was a hindrance. She sat back on her heels and reached for her handbag, fishing inside it until she found two elastic bands. Using her fingers as a comb, she pulled her hair back and secured it with the bands. Then she got down on all fours and tried to crawl underneath the sink.

'Bugger it!' she yelled, rubbing her forehead.

She tried again. Her arms stretched out as far as they would go, she extended her fingers, not daring to believe what they were suddenly feeling.

How old must she have been when she had seen her grandad do this? It had only been the once and he had made a joke of it, something about dripping pipes that she mustn't let her mother know about because it would only worry her. Something had jolted Carla's memory during the night, and now she was sure she had found Grandad's secret hiding place. The only question was, what had he hidden there?

She reached in as far as she could, and flexed her fingers until she was grasping whatever was in there. When she was sure her grip was secure, she gave a hefty tug.

It was a wooden box, dirty and dusty and covered in cobwebs. At one time it might have been wrapped in a brown paper bag, but after all these years, that covering was in shreds, mainly due to mice, Carla supposed. She hadn't the time to examine it now. She grabbed a paper carrier bag that was hanging from a hook on the door and quickly bundled it up, then shoved it in her handbag.

She gave the scullery floor a quick clean, then went back along the street to join the rest of the women. How amazing that whatever Grandad had hidden away so carefully hadn't been dislodged even by the German bombs, she thought. But why on earth had he never so much as mentioned it?

Peggy was getting ready to go shopping with Brenda when Carla walked in.

'Come with us if you like,' Brenda offered.

'Is the local library still open?' Carla asked.

'Yes, but why do you want to go there?'

'I haven't been sleeping too well and so I read in bed, but I didn't bring a book with me. Have any of you got a library card?'

'I have,' Brenda quickly offered. 'Come with us and I'll dig it out of my handbag.'

Fifteen minutes later, the three women were standing outside the library.

'Shall I come in with you?' Peggy offered.

'No, you were all set to go with Brenda. You can pick me up on the way back.'

'All right then, we shouldn't be too long.'

Once she was alone, Carla went to the back of the library, where a couple of tables and chairs were set out. This end of the room was quiet, with only two gentlemen seated at a table near the far wall. She removed the box from her handbag and laid it on the table in front of her. It smelt a bit musty. She was thankful that no one was sitting nearby.

The clasp clicked open quite easily. As she had expected, the box was full of papers with a yellowish tinge. Lying on top of the pile was a booklet with PREMIUM RECEIPT BOOK, PRUDENTIAL INSURANCE printed on the front in large letters. Next there were two sheaves of paper, both headed, ROYAL LIVER ASSURANCE.

Carla sighed. Grandad, you wise old bird, she thought. Did you have to be so secretive, though? All these years and you never let on what you had buried beneath that sink.

It seemed to Carla that just at that moment, her grandad was very close by. What had caused her to suddenly remember something that must have happened more than twenty years ago? She couldn't help feeling that he was watching over her, making sure that all would be well.

I love you dearly, Grandad, she told him silently. Always have. Always will. God bless you.

Chapter 22

It was now eight o'clock in the evening, and once more, every member of the family was assembled at Jack and Edna's house. Arthur had been included in the invitation because Carla felt that if anyone knew what to do with the papers she had unearthed it would be him.

Her uncles had all looked through the contents of the box, but no one had an opinion on what should happen next, and silence hung heavy in the room.

'Would it be best if we took everything to a solicitor and let them sort out just what is what?' This came from Albert, usually the quietest of the three.

'Arthur, do you mind telling us what you think?'

asked Jack. 'You own your own property and have had dealings with a solicitor. We do need a bit of guidance.'

'If you are all happy for me to do so, then yes, I will gladly offer you my advice.' Arthur had spoken very softly.

Three heads quickly nodded.

'Well, the first priority is to get at least two copies of your father's death certificate to take to the companies with whom he appears to have held insurance policies. I do not think you are going to have much trouble; everything I have looked at seems to be valid. Trouble is, in cases like this the wheels grind slowly and it will take time before these policies will be paid out. However, you will be given proof of ownership when you hand in the documents, and that will be security enough for any firm.

'I have looked through both the policies, but I am no expert and can't tell you what they are worth. They were obviously taken out many years ago, and there will also undoubtedly be bonuses to be added.'

'One last question, please, Arthur.' This request had come from Albert.

'All right, but it has been a very long day, so let's make it quick.' Arthur sounded determined.

'It appears that Carla has unearthed two policies. Can you tell us what the difference is?'

'Yes, that's an easy one. An insurance policy is a binding contract, paid out in case of loss, damage or death. The second policy is an assurance policy; that means payment *only* on death. Your father was a wise man. He covered every angle.'

Arthur felt that if they stayed any longer, they would just be going round in circles, so he signalled to Brenda and said, 'Shall I walk you, Carla and Peggy up the street?' Looking round the room, he added, 'I think we have done all we can for today, but before we break up, how about everyone saying thank you to Carla. These documents she found will save the family a whole lot of heartache, and will be of untold value in the long run.'

Everyone in the room gave Carla a hug, and all of them were loud in their praise for her initiative. Despite this upbeat end to the evening, however, it was a subdued and thoughtful trio that Arthur accompanied home.

Just three days later, Arthur was having a morning cup of coffee with Brenda, Carla and Peggy. A sudden hearty laugh made all three women stare at him

'Sorry,' Arthur said, still sounding very cheerful. 'There has never been a truer statement than "money speaks all languages".' He reached into his briefcase and withdrew a bundle of papers. 'Just the mention of the policies and also a lump sum from Grandad's pension have greased the wheels for us, and we now have the go-ahead on every last item. Jack and Albert have gone to court to pick up all the permits we need, and then you will all be able to breathe out and arrange to lay your grandad to rest at last.'

The three women all let out a deep sigh of relief.

Wanting all loose ends covered, Arthur pressed on. 'Carla, tomorrow the churchyard custodians will be opening up your mother's grave so that Grandad can be buried with her as he wanted. You are not to worry; the space will be covered straight away with a blanket of green turf, which will remain in place until the day of the funeral.

'Now to the actual funeral. Your uncles have ordered four horse-drawn carriages, clear windows on each side. The service itself will be up to you women; the prayers and hymns will also be your choice. After the service, the family and close friends will go to the graveside. Prayers will be said, flowers may be laid. After that short service, Grandad's coffin will be lowered and wreaths laid out.

'All three of his sons have done their best. They have already instructed that as soon as things have settled down, new turf is to be laid over what will now be a family grave, and they have certainly made Brenda happy. Will you tell them, Brenda, or shall I?'

'I will,' Brenda said softly. 'The men have agreed that after Grandad's funeral is over, they are going to have my Fred's name inscribed on a new tombstone, along with the details of how he died. It has pleased me so much, for my Joseph's sake especially, and I have you to thank for the suggestion, Arthur.'

Arthur smiled. 'If our Carla had not had that midnight conversation with her grandfather, God above knows there would have been a very different story for this family to sort out.' He looked at Carla. 'If I am ever in deep trouble, please have a word with the gods on my behalf, or if they are too busy, try your grandad for me, because that man was a genius if ever there was one.'

The day of the funeral had arrived and everyone thanked God that the weather was fine. The turnout was unbelievable! On every road, every street corner, folk had gathered. At twelve o'clock, a cannon was fired within the bounds of the Port of London.

'It is wonderful that the company are showing such respect for our dad,' his sons agreed. But then their father had worked in the dockyards from the day he had turned fourteen years old.

Even the traffic seemed quiet as the beautiful grey horses drew the carriage taking Grandad on his last earthly journey, his coffin covered in floral tributes. All the way along the route folk were showing their respect. Men removed their hats and women were saying a silent prayer. The church was packed, with dozens standing at the back.

Grandad's young grandsons had been told that he was going to heaven to meet with their grandma and aunt and so many other good friends. The boys had been allowed to choose the first hymn. It was one they had learnt in Sunday school: 'All Things Bright and Beautiful'. The singing brought tears to the eyes of a good many folk. Carla felt her Uncle

Jack take hold of her hand, and Albert handed her a clean white handkerchief.

The most moving part of the day was when the entire family gathered around her mother's graveside. Now Grandad was to be laid to rest with her.

Much later that day, when everything had settled down, Carla asked her uncles a question that had been worrying her for some time.

'Please, will one of you explain to me why Grandma is in a grave on her own, almost alongside the one that now holds both my mother and Grandad.'

Several voices were quick to answer. 'Money was in very short supply at that time, and a family plot would have cost a fortune.' Enough said.

Arthur played the peacemaker. 'It's great that they are now all so close together, and several of the floral arrangements today were laid on your grandma's grave.'

The whole family were happy with that.

One way and another it had been a long, sad day. Goodnights were said and the family dispersed to their own homes.

'Before I say goodnight, I'd like to make a suggestion,' Arthur said, not waiting for an answer. 'Carla, all three of your uncles have got the day off tomorrow, and they have offered to come up to my place and see if we can decide what to do on the house next. We have been making great progress, but decisions need to be made now, and since you expressed a wish to see the house before you and Peggy go home, I thought we could make a day of it.'

'Thank you, Arthur – great idea – I really would like to see what you've done to the place, and a day such as you suggest means we would all part on a far happier note.'

Turning to face Peggy, she asked, 'How does that sound to you? We aren't in such a desperate hurry to get back to work that one more day will make a difference.'

'No, of course, you're right. Besides, I have been longing to see what progress all the men have made.'

'Good, that's settled then,' said Arthur. 'I hope you have a good night's sleep and I shall see all of you in the morning.'

Carla and Peggy exchanged glances, then the two of them discreetly made their way up to bed, leaving Brenda and Arthur to themselves.

Chapter 23

Early next morning, there was so much coming and going that Carla almost wished she and Peggy had not decided to stay on. Her uncles had parked their vans outside in the street. The six boys were becoming impatient; they loved being let loose in the grounds of Uncle Arthur's big house, and after the past days, which had been so sad, they were delighted to be offered the chance of freedom.

The lads were all aboard, and now it only remained for the women to climb in wherever they could find a space. Both Carla and Peggy looked bewildered when Arthur's car turned the corner and he sounded the hooter twice. Thankfully, they made their way along the road and climbed into the back of the car. Brenda sat in the front next to Arthur.

'I bet you're thinking that you've bitten off more than you can chew this morning,' Peggy declared.

Arthur smiled. 'I guessed something like this might happen and that is why I am here to help with the transporting.' He straightened the mirror over the dashboard and caught Brenda's eye. 'Bit of a squash this morning, but as the day goes on I'm hoping everyone will think it has been worth the effort. Oh, and while I am about it, I may as well bring you up to date. Some time ago I found a couple who had been made homeless through no fault of their own. I set them up in two rooms that hadn't been too much affected by bomb damage, and they both now work for me. Mr Patterson turns his hand to a great many jobs, whilst his wife is a darn good cook, as you will notice the minute you set foot in the kitchen.'

It was such a short journey, there was no time for more talk.

All three vanloads had arrived safely, and the youngsters were already running here, there and everywhere.

Even the drive leading up to the house looked very different to Carla. A new, smooth surface had been laid, and the hedges and trees that ran alongside had all been trimmed. The oak front door stood half open. It had been waxed, and the knocker and other brass fittings absolutely gleamed. What a difference since that day when she had first sat down on the stone steps.

'Don't just stand there,' Arthur laughed. He had

known that Carla of all people would remember the state this house and grounds had been in when they had first discovered each other. 'Come and see the kitchen, though first, in your mind's eye, draw yourself a picture of everything as it was when you first entered this house.'

Carla looked up at him and smiled as she linked her arm through his.

Through the huge entrance hall, with its massive high ceiling, and now the walls were a sight to behold. Dear Jesus, what a transformation! They were covered from floor to ceiling in carved wooden panels.

She could hear voices as Arthur held the kitchen door open. A very tall man, with a skin that said he lived most of his life outdoors, stood beside a lady with a starched white cook's hat on her head and a white overall wrapped tightly around her. The woman moved over to the fireplace, lifted the lid from a very large saucepan and began to stir the contents. The very smell had Carla feeling hungry, and more so when the woman turned to her and said, 'I do hope you all like your soup thick, 'cos this is vegetable and there's no shortage of them on this land now.'

Carla couldn't resist looking around. There were so many pots and saucepans, all tidily hung up on hooks on the walls. The flagstone floor was shiny-clean, but what engaged her interest the most was the enormous fireplace and the crackling flames that leaped and roared up the big chimney. She couldn't resist sniffing, and her mouth watered as she inhaled the strong smell of freshly baked bread.

She turned towards Arthur. 'It has always been said that one good turn deserves another, and you seem to have struck really lucky to have found such help.'

'True, very true,' Arthur said. 'Let me introduce you. This is Mr Patterson, who has proved that he is able to tackle almost any job that needs doing, and this is his wife, who is responsible for reclaiming this kitchen and bringing it back to life.'

Arthur turned around and drew Carla to his side. 'And this is the person that I found sitting outside on the cold steps one morning many months ago.'

'I am very pleased to meet both of you,' Carla said as she shook hands with them in turn.

That was just the beginning of a day that would live in the minds of every member of the Schofield family for a very long time.

The men all had some useful job to do, while Jack, Thomas, Joseph, Alan, John and David were having the time of their lives, dragging great branches across the ground and tossing them as best they could on to the several piles that were dotted about the garden. Uncle Arthur had already promised that when Guy Fawkes night came, they would come here for fireworks and a massive bonfire.

Meanwhile, the women were feeling a bit useless. Mrs Patterson had refused all offers of help in the kitchen. That was, until the clock showed almost one o'clock, when she called from the doorway that there were some folding tables and a few chairs in the nearest shed.

'The men will be fine sitting on the ground, but place all the tables together and then I would appreciate some help with bringing out the hot food.'

The women did their best to hide their smiles. Despite the fact that they were not used to being told what to do, they were all enjoying the day.

Within half an hour, Carla could not entirely believe the transformation. The tables were all erected and, covered with snow-white linen tablecloths, they looked like one long dining table. The boys had been sent to find the menfolk and to tell them to come now because the hot food was ready to be served.

No one needed telling twice!

The men washed their hands at the outside tap and Mr Patterson put on a white apron with a high bib. His wife took the apron strings and tied them into a bow at the back. Then the convoy of food to the table began. Bowls of thick soup were followed by sizzling sausages for the children and several large meat pies for the adults. The final dishes laid out were greeted with great cheers and laughter from the Schofield lads: they were full of piping-hot chips.

Carla looked along the line of happy faces seated across from each other, and she silently thanked God for this day and for the kindness that Arthur had shown to all the family. The sadness of losing Grandad had not faded, but today had proved a good tonic for the young ones and their parents.

She would add this day to her memories, though it would have been a hundred per cent better if Paul could have been here with her. She had found it hard to come to terms with the fact that his letters never arrived regularly. Periodically several airmail letters would arrive together, but they never said where he was. They always had to go through a postal drop. She often wondered whether he was being moved to different hospitals for special treatment. But with no friends who knew his whereabouts or any relatives in this country, there was nothing she could do except keep writing.

By five o'clock, the men agreed that it was time the boys were taken home. A noisy departure had those left up in the big house in fits of laughter. The boys had almost demanded written permission to come and visit whenever the mood took them.

Peggy and Carla helped Mrs Patterson with the washing-up, while Brenda gave Mr Patterson a hand stowing away all the garden furniture. Joseph was sleeping at his cousin Alan's house tonight.

'Well,' sighed Peggy as she and Carla stood outside on the steps.

'Well what?' Carla laughed.

'Where do we go from here?' Peggy queried.

'Back to the grindstone, first thing tomorrow

morning. There will be plenty of post waiting to be sorted, I'd lay money on that. Oh, and another thing we need to do is chase up the installation of the ruddy telephone, which the company promised to do nearly a month ago.'

'Lots of memories we've made these past few days, haven't we?' Peggy said.

'We surely have, and you've been a real brick, but right now Arthur is flashing the headlights of his car, which means he is ready to take us home to pick up our suitcases.'

'Is Brenda coming with us or is she staying here?'

'Peggy, I have no idea what is happening between her and Arthur, and I'm not going to ask questions.'

'Well I suppose we shall find out soon, especially if we get the phone laid on.'

Carla took a deep breath. 'The telephone is supposed to be a business line, a sheer necessity.'

Peggy looked disappointed, but she knew she had better keep quiet.

As Carla climbed into the back seat, Arthur turned his head and said, 'Everybody seemed to enjoy themselves, and that is good. However, I meant to take you up to the first floor of the house, where both the family dining room and the main lounge have been renovated. I am so pleased with the result that I shall soon be thinking about refurbishing the rest of that part of the house. When the time comes, Carla, I would very much value your advice.'

'Oh Arthur, why didn't you mention this earlier

in the day? I would dearly love to see what improvements you have made.'

'I couldn't help but notice that you were impressed with the ground floor, especially the kitchen.'

'Well who wouldn't be? I think you did well to engage Mr and Mrs Patterson, but I couldn't help but remember what the place was like the day you first invited me in.'

'Yes, we have come a long way since then, and I'm talking about both of us. You have certainly mastered the art of being your own boss, and now, with your first major wedding under your belt, you are all set to climb the ladder of success.'

'I couldn't have done it without you, Arthur. You stood as guarantor for all my loans; nobody else would have done that. You've been truly responsible for setting me up in business.'

'Well just keep climbing that ladder, and I shall reap my reward.' His voice was full of emotion, and Carla's eyes were brimming with tears as she moved to the other side of the back seat, leaving room for Peggy to get in beside her.

Once they had picked up their luggage from Brenda's house, it wasn't long before they were drawing up outside the two massive buildings that the girls now called home. The eyes of both were immediately drawn to their working area, their first thought, as always, one of relief that their precious sewing machines were still securely covered and the bales of material lying in orderly fashion on the shelves that had been set up along the far wall.

Now to the post! The doormat was literally covered, their first glance telling them that there were at least two copies of last week's paper, which undoubtedly held photographs of the wedding. They had to be patient, sort everything out before they decided which job was to come first.

'One here from the GPO; must be about the telephone being installed,' Peggy called across to where Carla was contentedly clutching three airmail letters, which had to be from Paul.

'If one of you would pick up the rest of the post and the other one put the kettle on and make us all a hot drink, then there's a chance I might get home before midnight.' Arthur spoke in a stern voice, but there was a twinkle in his eye.

'I'll make the tea,' Peggy offered.

'Thank God for that.' Arthur paused. 'Now that I have a few moments alone with you, Carla, will you tell me how things are between you and Paul?'

'If there was anything to tell, you would be the first to know. He writes quite regularly, but there is never a proper return address.'

'I suppose one could put that down to the possibility that the operation on his ankle has not been straightforward. It has more than likely involved more than one surgeon, which will have meant travelling to various places.'

'That is what I tell myself over and over again,' Carla said.

Arthur leaned forward. 'From everything you've told me, it seems that Paul is a fine, upstanding young man. He wanted to be more than just a friend from the moment he set eyes on you, but with that ankle always holding him back, he felt it wasn't fair to spoil your chances. The reason he agreed to go to America was because the operation gave him the prospect of a normal life. Just keep writing to him, Carla, and do your best to be patient.'

'Please will one of you clear all that post from the table so that I can set this heavy tea tray down,' Peggy said as she came into the room.

Arthur stood up and did as Peggy had asked, and soon they were all drinking tea and nibbling biscuits.

Half an hour later, the girls were once more out at the front waving goodbye to their dear friend.

'I am so glad that Arthur asked the family to spend the day up at his house. It lessened the sadness of burying Grandad,' Carla said. 'Now we have to roll up our sleeves and get cracking. Sort the post first. Tidy things up, do our personal bits of washing, later maybe do a bit of shopping to fill some of the shelves in the larder, and from then on it's noses to the sewing machines.'

'We've still got a good stock of materials, and I'm longing to read our mail to see if there are any prospects of new orders,' Peggy replied.

Carla was pleased that Peggy was being optimistic, though she herself suspected that it would take at least two days for them to get back into a steady working routine.

'Let's get moving then, and make a start,' she said. She pulled Peggy to her feet, and the two friends hugged each other.

Chapter 24

It had been a month since Grandad's funeral, and Peggy and Carla were more than pleased with the way their work had been accepted in so many different outlets. Carla felt that she owed a particular debt to Mr Ainsley, editor of the local paper. The wedding photographs that had been published in the weekly edition were really good, and the write-up that the reporter had filed had been worth its weight in gold.

It was almost unbelievable just how far their reputation had spread in such a short time. It had been a godsend having the telephone connected. Quite a few well-known firms had approached Carla requesting samples, with a promise of a contract for further orders should the samples prove to be popular.

Smaller firms had asked whether she would consider contracts for alterations to customers' purchases. She had given a lot of thought to this matter, fully aware that a short while ago she would have jumped at the chance. But now she felt she was in a position to turn down such work.

Last evening they had received two phone calls asking for details for bridal gowns and bridesmaids' dresses. Both callers had been told that they must come in person to discuss their requirements before any costs could be worked out.

For two whole weeks there had been no let-up, with both girls giving work their full attention. Then at midnight the night before, Carla had declared that enough was enough and it was time for bed. This morning they had taken it in turns to lie in the bath. The hot, scented water had been sheer luxury.

It was Peggy who had suggested they each try on a dress or a suit and parade in it so as to see what the other thought of the finished article. Apart from Peggy being about an inch taller than Carla, their measurements were almost identical.

Peggy came out of their bedroom. She had no shoes on, and her face was only lightly made up, but it glowed with health, as did her eyes. Her hair was brushed and gleaming. The two-piece suit she was wearing was a credit to them both – there could be little doubt that it would become a favourite. Young office workers would scrimp and save to buy such a smart outfit. Navy blue always looked good, and

185

combined with crisp and immaculate white, it would sell like hot cakes.

Now it was Carla's turn. On this special morning, with their hard work having achieved such good results, she was filled with high hopes for the future. She had gone the extra mile and was wearing a floor-length evening gown. The basic colour was a very pale peach, and all the buttons and buckles were silver. The neckline crossed her bust but continued over one shoulder only, leaving the other bare, and there was a slit at the side that rose to calf-length, which would make dancing in this dress quite perfect.

Everything having worked out so well, they both felt they were due for a treat and decided to go out for lunch. As they set foot in the café, congratulations came at them from all sides. It seemed that everyone must have read the local paper.

With melon as a starter and fresh salmon to follow, both Peggy and Carla were beginning to unwind and relax. They ate in silence until they reached the coffee stage. Then Peggy looked straight at Carla and quietly asked, 'If I work my socks off for the next three weeks, would you mind if I took a fortnight's holiday?'

'Of course not, Peggy, God knows you deserve it. Have you any idea as to where you will go?

At that moment the waitress placed a bowl of tinned peaches in front of each of them, along with a jug of fresh cream. That kept them occupied for a while.

Once she had scraped her bowl clean, Peggy said,

'I am not thinking of going on holiday as such. I would just like to go home. Being with your family made me realise that I've been neglecting my own.'

'Now you are making me feel guilty,' Carla said. 'I love having you with me but now I'm thinking I have been a bit selfish. You make your arrangements and that will be fine by me.'

Both girls relaxed. They were enjoying this good life they had worked out for themselves, and the way they had prospered was the best possible outcome. They were making good money, and work was being offered to them from so many different quarters that they still were finding it hard to believe it.

In fact Carla had given some thought as to whether it might be a good idea to take on a couple of apprentices. That would certainly ease the load. More especially if they could find youngsters who had some experience in the basics, such as tacking seams and hems.

The more thought she gave to this idea, the more feasible it became. Still burning with ambition, she told herself there was no reason why she should not become an employer. Within the next week she was due to visit the solicitor that Arthur had introduced her to. She had no intention of taking this next step without first seeking legal advice. There would be so many pitfalls, she had to be sure that everything was done by the book. She would talk to Arthur first, and if he thought it was a good idea, then she would take it further.

★

Three days later, she was sitting waiting for Arthur to arrive to take her to the solicitor's. As always, he arrived on time, looking immaculate in a charcoal-coloured three-piece suit, a pristine white shirt and a deep red striped silk tie. Even his black leather shoes shone. All of which was no surprise to Carla. As time had passed, she had become aware of the different personas that he could so easily adopt.

The solicitor's offices were in the West End. The building was very old, but the interior reeked of wealth. Every member of staff treated Carla with the utmost courtesy, but despite their efforts, she never really felt at ease.

Anthony Nichols greeted them both warmly and listened carefully to what Carla had to say. The look on his face was grave, and it was a full minute before he answered her.

'My first reaction is to tell you that as you are doing so well, leave the matter of staff for the time being. To be an employer will involve you in so much more paperwork. First question, do you make your own tax returns, or do you employ a firm of chartered accountants?'

Carla looked across at Arthur and then turned a sheepish look towards Mr Nichols. 'I don't think I have ever made a tax return.'

Both men struggled to keep a straight face.

'Well, young lady, you may well get away with it. I presume you do keep accounts, and as you have been trading for less than a year, there is not a great deal for you to worry about yet. However, my advice to you is to find yourself a decent accountant, and don't take on any staff unless you can't do without them.' At that moment a young, very businesslike woman entered the office carrying a tray which held three cups and saucers, a coffee pot and a cream jug. As she poured the coffee, Carla took in every detail of the smart navy-blue costume she was wearing. The jacket was double-breasted, which was most unusual for a ladies' suit, and she made a mental note of it.

On the way home, Carla wondered where on earth she would find a firm of accountants. She suspected that Arthur would know one. Now that she had been informed of the legalities she would come up against were she to employ staff, she wasn't so keen on the idea. She would let it drop, for the time being at least.

Survival had been the most important thing when she had started out, and she must not let herself get too greedy. Survival still mattered above all else.

Chapter 25

Realisation had just dawned on Carla: she was entirely on her own.

Standing in the doorway, she had watched until the taxi that was taking Peggy away to start her two weeks' holiday was out of sight. She remained silent and thoughtful for a few moments and then out loud she said, 'Stop being so miserable. You're on your own now, so what? It won't be for the first time.'

Having filled the kettle and lit the gas beneath it, she cleared the table of the remains of the breakfast that she and Peggy had shared. Now she was going to have a fresh cup of tea and then get down to some serious work.

Her week was well set out. Between Peggy and

herself, they had finished six sample garments. They had copied each garment twice, so that she now had eighteen to carefully pack up. Then via the telephone she would notify the three West End firms that their sample garments were ready for collection and the various vans would make the pick-up.

Eleven o'clock on the dot next morning and the front doorbell was ringing.

Carla opened the door and her face lit up.

'Hiya, Carla.' Edward Owen flashed her a wide smile, showing his perfect teeth, and took her outstretched hand, his clasp lingering. He was well over six feet tall, and well dressed, as he had to be, since he worked for Harrods. His tanned face and head of thick dark hair added to this fine figure of a man.

'Good morning, Edward, do please come in. The parcels are ready for you in the hall, but the kettle is on the boil if you would like a cup of tea or coffee.'

'I'd like a black coffee if that is all right by you, but please, first may I use your washroom.'

'Of course you may, you know where it is.'

Long ago Carla had come to the conclusion that she was unlucky in love. Then Paul had come into her life and she felt she had truly found the man for her. Why oh why had he had to disappear off to America so soon after they had met? To be honest, if it weren't for the fact that she really did love Paul, she might have looked twice at Eddie Owen. He was always so happy, never downhearted, and there were times when she could surely do with a nice evening out. But was he married? She had never asked.

She poured out a cup of black coffee, and at the very moment that Eddie sat down beside her, the doorbell rang again.

Eddie raised his eyebrows and smiled broadly. 'You must have the saints guarding you, Carla, to be saved from a brute like me by the doorbell.'

'Oh that *is* a pity,' she said. She was grinning as she left the kitchen to open the front door for the second time.

This time the van driver was not one that she had seen before, and he was nowhere near as friendly. He produced his identity card, and held his clipboard out for Carla's inspection.

'Yes, that is all in order,' she agreed. 'Three parcels, and you have a receipt for me, yes?'

'Yes, that is correct.'

She stepped back, opened the door wider and pointed to a stack of three parcels leaning against the wall. Without another word, he picked them up and carried them to his van.

As Carla came back into the kitchen, Eddie was laughing. 'What's tickling you?' she asked.

'Well it seems the magic you work on me and a couple more of the drivers I happen to know doesn't work on Serious Sam.'

'That's his loss then,' Carla answered sharply.

'I fully agree, especially because you do make a good cup of coffee.'

'Oh Eddie, so that's why you are so attentive towards me, is it? You're not in the least bit attracted to me, it's just that I make you a decent cup of coffee.'

'We won't go into details, but I have been picking up trade parcels from here for long enough to know that you are a lovely, dignified young lady, though I'm fully aware that you would put the shutters up if I were to ask you to allow me to take you out.'

Carla's face reddened, but she made no reply. Instead she poured herself a cup of coffee, topped up Eddie's cup and then sat herself down beside him.

It was Eddie who broke the silence. 'Peggy did tell me a few details about your friend Paul going to America. Whether you believe it or not, my wish for you is that he comes home to you soon. And if that's the case, I shall be looking for an invitation to your wedding, please.'

'Oh Eddie, you really are a very nice man, and if things do work out as I'd like them to, well of course I shall want you to be at my wedding.'

They finished their coffee, and as they both got to their feet, Eddie cleared his throat.

'I've written my telephone number on that receipt. If you feel in need of a bit of company while Peggy is away, just ring me. It won't take long for me to get down here.'

'Thank you, Eddie. I do appreciate that. Now I had better come and see you off, or else you'll be well behind with your deliveries.'

Not long after Eddie had driven away, the bell rang for the third time.

'Morning, Jeff,' Carla smiled. 'I'm always pleased when a pick-up or delivery is made by a driver I already know.'

'Why's that, Carla? Have you ever had a problem?'

'Not exactly, though some callers I do feel a bit wary of.'

'Quite right too,' Jeff Anderson said, offering his clipboard. 'Sign on the bottom of the sheet, please.'

Carla checked that the details were correct and scribbled her signature, then said, 'Jeff, would you like a cup of something?'

Jeff smiled regretfully. 'Carla, I'm relieved that you trust me enough to ask and I do appreciate the offer, but this time I am going to ask if I may take a rain-check. I've a full load on today and I can't afford to get behind.'

'I do understand, Jeff. I'll look forward to seeing you soon,' Carla said, stepping aside so that he could come into the hall and pick up his three packages.

When Jeff had left, Carla made for the workroom. As she switched on the electricity and started up her sewing machine, she heard the clatter of the letter box. She went to the door and picked the post up from the mat. Among the business correspondence were two airmail letters. She would leave Paul's letters until this evening, probably read them in bed. It would make her feel closer to him.

The rest of the post was mostly bills and orders, but there was also a letter from a Mr Gerald Bobbin, who owned two cotton mills in Blackburn, Lancashire. Carla read it twice, then folded it and replaced it in the envelope.

Mr Bobbin had fallen on hard times. Unknown to him, his business partner had been embezzling the firm's money over several years. By the time Mr Bobbin realised what had been happening, his partner had fled the country. Bobbin was now about to be declared bankrupt. Because Carla had been a customer, he was making her a good proposition. His premises and his machinery had all been sold, but he had been left with large stocks of cotton and woollen material.

Carla sighed. Of course she would help in any way she could, but the small amount of stock she could afford to purchase would go nowhere near to saving Mr Bobbin from bankruptcy.

It was with a heavy heart that she cleared her desk and made ready to start work.

Chapter 26

By bedtime, Carla's mood had lightened. She had read and reread Paul's letters, and at last he had told her that he would soon be leaving America and heading for home. This was the most loving letter he had written to her.

I long to hold you, I need to kiss you several times before I shall realise that you are truly in my arms. So many times have I imagined this homecoming. Just to look at you will suit me to begin with, then I shall need to put my arms around you and hold you tight.

I can't help wondering just how you have put up with me for so long.

The first operation was not successful. In fact I felt

more pain than I had previously. My ankle throbbed and felt burning hot all the time. Then I was advised to have a special scan at one of America's new orthopaedic hospitals, and it was there that it was discovered that the pain was coming from the shin bone as well as part of the ankle bone because the cartilage had worn away, so these bones had been rubbing together.

Please, Carla, will you marry me as soon as I reach home? I just could not stand the agony if you were to say that we must wait a while. Do you feel as I do? That we have known each other long enough to be fully aware that we are meant for one another? Carla, time and time again I have yearned to stop the operations, just up and come home. Then I have had to repeatedly tell myself that it would not be fair on you, being married to a cripple. You probably don't realise just how much my twisted ankle held me back. So many times I have wanted to hold you in my arms, but now, thank God, perseverance has paid off and I shall be eternally grateful to the surgeons who have been responsible for the operations.

I can't tell you how much I want to get back to my life – our life – in England. Being accepted as part of your family, doing all the little things that families do together spending Christmas with you all.

But I am getting ahead of myself. I shall close this letter now but end with some wonderful-sounding words.

My darling Carla, I shall be seeing you soon. Until then, all my love, God bless, Paul xxxx

For the tenth time, Carla reread that letter. Then, carefully folding it, she held it against her cheek.

Was it really true? All that endless waiting would soon be over. When would his aircraft land? Oh, how badly she wanted to be there to meet him. Did she remember just how tall and good-looking he was? Would he be able to pick her out in the crowds?

For goodness' sake stop it, she told herself. Paul would send a telegram when his travel arrangements were complete, Thank you, dear God, she murmured over and over again.

Peggy had been gone for five days now, and Carla was feeling lonely. She had started work at seven o'clock in the morning and barely stopped for something to eat, let alone a rest, until she wound things up at six in the evening. Having covered her sewing machine, she walked away from work and into the second building, which had become a cosy refuge.

First things first, she grinned to herself as she half-filled the kettle and placed it on the stove to boil. She did realise that there wasn't any need for her to keep working quite so hard. She had plenty of contracts now, and money in the bank. But the desire to work hard and do well for herself was in her blood – it was the way she had been brought up. Sometimes it seemed as if everything she touched turned out well, but she knew it wasn't all down to luck. She loved sewing and she had worked hard to put her ideas into being, but now that Paul was coming home, she'd slow down, make time to spend with him.

The future suddenly seemed a whole lot brighter.

Carla worked steadily all the following day, leaving her place at her sewing machine only when she needed to go to the lavatory or to fetch herself a glass of water.

When she did eventually lean back and stretch both arms way up high above her head, her wristwatch told her it was a quarter past seven. 'I'm not a bit hungry,' she said out loud, 'but I could do with a breath of fresh air.' She walked towards the window and looked out. It was a pitch-black night, not a star in the sky and no wind as far as she could tell. Paul was right. Christmas wasn't far off, and how wonderful it would be to spend it together. A stroll into the village would blow the cobwebs away, and she might even pick up some fish and chips.

Once she had made her mind up, she got cracking, pulling on her old duffel coat and winding a long woolly scarf around her neck.

She had scarcely turned the key in the door than she heard an almighty thud. So loud was the sound that had echoed right through the building that even now she could still feel the reverberation beneath her feet.

'Oh my God!' she cried. She stepped out into the dark and ran towards the back of the buildings. She saw instantly that a huge lorry had driven right into the brick wall.

She couldn't see any movement in the cab of the lorry, and she was just about to go back inside and telephone for an ambulance when someone grabbed her arm and yanked her forward, pulling her scarf from around her neck, pushing and shoving her past the lorry. The outside light had come on – it must have been when the lorry hit the wall – and Carla could see that her assailant was a large, bedraggled man, overweight and stinking of drink. He tightened his hold and slammed her against the wall.

'You're the clever bitch that bought these two buildings, aren't you?'

Before she could form an answer, he tightened his grip on her shoulders and shook her hard.

'I've been in bleeding prison because of you. You think when it comes to business you're the smart one who knows it all. Well we'll see about that, shall we?' His breath was so foul it made Carla heave. 'For years I rented these buildings to keep my lorries in. Then what 'appens? Our lord and master ups the rent, and when I can't pay, he sells off both proper-ties to a bloody slip of a girl. Never mind that you put me out of business.'

'I think I read about you in the local paper,' Carla said, far more calmly than she felt. 'But that all happened before I had even seen the buildings. You owed more than two years' rent, and the court ordered you to clear the debt or vacate the property.'

She knew immediately that she had overstepped the mark. She had waved a red rag in the face of a man with a grudge who was also very drunk. He grabbed her hair and banged her head hard against the wall behind her, then drew his fist back and slammed it into the side of her head.

Everything went dim and blurry for an instant, and Carla started to slide down the rough brickwork. She felt this horrible man kick her twice, and the second kick was directed straight at her stomach. Then he punched her full in the face and she fell to the ground.

She lay still, praying that he would leave her alone now, but then his boot thudded into her again and again, until the pain became too much to bear and she drifted into unconsciousness.

It was almost nine o'clock when two policemen doing their rounds saw that the light was on outside Miss Schofield's work premises. When they went to investigate, they immediately spotted a woman's body lying on the ground close to a massive lorry that had crashed quite spectacularly into one of the building's back walls.

One of the officers knelt down next to the woman and felt for a pulse, while the other called for an ambulance. When his colleague carefully stroked her hair away from her bloodied face, he exclaimed, 'Oh my God, it's Miss Schofield. I hardly recognised her, the state she's in.'

'Who on this earth could have laid into a young woman and then cleared off and left her like this?' his colleague asked.

His mate could only shake his head in disbelief.

The ambulance came within fifteen minutes. The attendants were quick to lift Carla on to a stretcher, and were giving her oxygen even as they slid her into the vehicle.

'She's a local lady, works and lives in this very building,' said one of the policemen. 'Any idea how bad she is?'

'She's taken a severe beating, but it's the head injuries that are the worst,' said the ambulance man. 'One of you will have to come with us; the doctors will need to know anything you can tell them.'

At the hospital, the constable followed the two doctors walking either side of the trolley that was taking Carla to a side room.

'She's a real mess,' one of the doctors said. 'Do you know what happened?'

'I can tell you for sure, this was no ordinary mugging, Doctor. We'll be after a bloke who is well known to us and has been recently released from prison. He left his lorry at the scene, which helps.'

An hour and a half later, the constables were reporting back to the officer in charge at the police station. It was well known locally that Carla's family lived in the East End, and the sergeant telephoned the station there to pass on the news.

'They'll send someone round to Miss Schofield's

relatives to let them know what has happened,' he said.

Every copper on duty that night knew full well how they themselves would feel if their daughter or niece were to be attacked so brutally. None of them would blame Carla Schofield's family for wanting revenge on the man responsible.

Chapter 27

Sid had his jacket on and was running up the street to find Jack and Albert almost before the police had finished telling him what had happened to Carla.

When they finally arrived en masse at the hospital, they were shown into a waiting room.

'How bad is she?' Jack ventured to ask one of the doctors.

'At this point in time her condition is critical, but you can be assured that she will receive the very best medical attention. At present, the doctors are patching her up, making her as comfortable as possible. Surgery will come later. You may be able to see her just for a minute or two; she is being transferred to a side ward, where she will have nurses in attendance round the clock. Then I suggest you all go home and come back again in the morning.'

By the time the three Schofield brothers were allowed into the side ward, their imaginations had run riot. They loved Carla dearly, and if she died, the man who had done this dreadful thing would be wishing that he could die too. That oath had been muttered by all three brothers.

Tough East Enders they certainly were, but as they tiptoed into the room, there was not a dry eye among them.

Carla was almost unrecognisable. Her poor face was misshapen and bruised, her eyes were swollen shut and her head was swathed in bandages. Her beautiful hair had had to be cut away in places and now looked an utter mess. Her right arm was broken and several ribs had been strapped up, but it was the injuries to her head that were causing the doctors most concern.

Once outside the room again, the three brothers just had to vent their pent-up anger.

'That bastard is going to wish he had never been born,' Albert declared forcefully.

'You're not kidding,' Sid joined in. 'We'll make sure he suffers every minute of what he put our Carla through. Killing is too bloody good for that son of a bitch.'

Next morning all four of Carla's aunts were at the hospital by eleven o'clock. They were ushered into a side room and asked to wait.

As the door closed, the silence felt heavy. They were all dreading having to see Carla after the men had relayed to them just what had happened.

Time was dragging when two women wearing flowered overalls opened the door and pushed a large tea trolley into the room.

'Would you ladies like a hot drink? We have tea or coffee,' said the older of the two, while the other lady was setting out four cups and saucers.

Mary, Brenda, Edna and Daisy answered as one. 'Cup of tea, please.'

The tea was good and hot, which was more than they had expected. Edna finished hers, and put the cup loudly back on to the saucer. 'How much longer before they allow us to see our Carla? I'm getting worried that something's wrong.'

'I'm sure we'll hear soon, one way or the other,' Daisy promised, and the words were hardly out of her mouth when the door opened and a gentleman wearing a very smart dark grey suit came in.

'I am Dr Bannister, one of the medical team that is taking care of Miss Schofield. I understand you are all relatives.'

'Yes, we are,' Mary answered.

'I am sorry, but you won't be able to see Miss Schofield today.'

There was uproar as they all spoke together.

'Why not?' 'Has she taken a turn for the worse?' 'What's happened?'

'Ladies, please. Some of Miss Schofield's injuries

have already been dealt with, but the more severe injuries need surgery and she has been taken down to the operating theatre. Let us hope that we get better news later on in the day.'

The women apologised, and Brenda added, 'But thank you for coming to tell us.'

When the doctor had left, they finished their tea in silence. They were all sad at having to leave the hospital without seeing Carla, but they knew they had no choice.

The plane bringing Paul Robinson home to England landed at London Airport early that afternoon. He booked into a hotel and tried telephoning Carla at her work premises, but got no reply. There was one other place that he could try.

At half past six a taxi turned into Tilbury Terrace and Paul got out. He paid the driver, adding a good tip, then stepped on to the pavement and knocked on the door of Carla's family home.

The door was opened by Arthur, who looked the visitor over with interest. Handsome young man, well dressed, and his voice and accent were a surprise when he introduced himself as Paul Robinson. Arthur immediately held out his hand, drawing Paul over the doorstep.

'I'm afraid we have bad news,' he said. 'Our Carla is in hospital.'

Paul felt his blood run cold. 'What's happened? How bad is she?'

Arthur hesitated. 'Last night she was brutally beaten by the thug who used to rent her business premises. We don't know all the details yet, only that Carla is in a terrible state. The man was drunk and he must have been out of his mind the way he laid into her.'

'Have any of you been allowed to see her?' Paul asked.

'Her uncles saw her last night, but she's been in the operating theatre today.'

'Which hospital is she in?' Paul's voice shook as he asked the question

'She was taken to St Thomas's.' Arthur looked at Paul, and immediately felt sorry for him. He looked so tired. 'When did your plane touch down?'

'Earlier this afternoon. I booked into a hotel and came straight here.'

'I've got a better idea. Come home with me. I expect Carla has told you about my house in her letters. It's got a long way to go to being finished, but parts of it are habitable and you will be able to use the telephone to ring the hospital.'

'Carla has often told me what a good friend you are, and for the time being, if you are sure I shall not be a hindrance, I shall gladly accept your kind offer.'

'Good, that's settled. We can collect your luggage tomorrow; for tonight I am sure I can supply you with anything you need. Right now I think you must be in need of a drink.'

'How did you guess? A cup of coffee would go down well.'

Brenda had heard this and she quickly smiled and said, 'I'll get it for you.'

'Is there anything I can do for Carla at the moment?' Paul asked.

'Only what we've been doing all day long. Pray,' Arthur told him sadly.

Once they were at Arthur's house, Paul sat down by the telephone with a pen and notepad that Arthur had handed to him. He picked up the phone with a sudden sick feeling in his stomach.

'Yes, hallo Doctor, my name is Paul Robinson. I only arrived from America a few hours ago. My fiancée is Carla Elizabeth Schofield, who I under-stand has been admitted to your hospital. What can you tell me about her condition?'

Dr Bannister introduced himself before informing Paul that there was not a great deal he could tell him at this point.

Tears were pricking Paul's eyes as he whispered into the phone, 'We were aiming to be married within the next few weeks. May I come and see her?'

'Yes, of course, but you must be aware of the fact that she is going into intensive care when she leaves surgery. As yet it is hard to say whether she will pull through. She has youth on her side and most of her injuries should heal pretty well. Her head is another matter. It has been decided that brain surgery is not an option. Only time will tell; we just have to be patient. Meanwhile, I can guarantee that everything that can be done for your fiancée will be undertaken by the best medical specialists.'

'Thank you, I shall be there shortly,' Paul murmured as he replaced the receiver.

Arthur was shaking his head. 'You have had enough shocks for one day, but if you insist on going to the hospital right now, I shall take you.'

Paul's voice trembled as he answered. 'I won't get through the night if I can't see her.'

The short journey was a silent one, and in no time at all they were standing side by side at the enquiry desk in the main reception hall of St Thomas's Hospital.

'Dr Bannister has given us permission to have a few minutes with his patient Miss Carla Schofield.' Paul spoke in barely a whisper to the nurse behind the desk.

'I was expecting you, Mr Robinson. An orderly is standing by the lift to take you up to her ward.'

'Thank you so much.' It was Arthur who answered. Paul was shaking from head to toe.

As the two men walked into the small ward, it would have been impossible to decide which of them was the more upset. Paul knelt down at the side of the bed. It was a minute or two before he found his voice.

'My darling Carla, I am back in England. I want you to be better quickly. We have a church service to arrange, and at that service you will become my wife.' He squeezed her hand. 'I shall leave you now and pray hard that you get a good night's rest. First thing in the morning I shall be back, and from now on there will not be a single day that I shall not see you. I just have to keep on reminding you that I fell in love with you on the very first day we met. Don't you go worrying about me. Arthur has taken me under his wing and the pair of us will make sure that you get better very soon. Goodnight, Carla my darling, I love you dearly, and we are going to spend every day of the rest of our lives together. For now try and sleep well.'

Arthur kneeled down beside the bed. He was so choked up at the sight of his beloved Carla that he couldn't bring himself to say a single word. Inside his head, though, he was pleading with his Heavenly Father. 'Dear Lord, you sent Carla to me when I was feeling lost and unwanted. She has certainly become the answer to my prayers. I love and cherish her as if she were my own daughter. Please don't take her from me now.'

Leaving Carla that night was the hardest thing those two men had ever had to do.

Over the following days, Paul spent hours by Carla's bedside. Injections had made her woozy, but at least she wasn't in quite as much pain. Looking at her dear face, so battered and bruised, was enough to break his heart. Every couple of days he brought her fresh flowers, which the nurses would put into a glass vase and place where Carla could see them.

One afternoon Paul was trying hard to get Carla to focus on him, telling her of their wedding arrangements, when suddenly she became fretful.

'What is it, my darling?' He stroked her hand gently, trying to calm her.

Carla managed a deep breath before she murmured, 'Paul, are you sure you still wish to marry me?'

That question really hurt him

'Carla, the state you are in is not in any way your fault. What that beast of a man did to you was unforgivable. What we have to do now is count our blessings.'

Carla blinked. 'What blessings?' she murmured.

Paul tried to stay calm. 'We are both alive and we are together after a very long absence. Most importantly, we still have a great love for each other. And I mean this. You and I are shortly going to be married. Husband and wife until death us do part. I wish it were possible to change places with you, to take all your aches and pains away. I love you so much and I am sorry as hell that you have had to suffer like this. But you are slowly recovering and you will soon become my wife. As long as we are together, I shall look after you, whatever it takes. How does that sound to you?'

'Oh Paul, I really do love you.'

'Well that goes for the pair of us then,' he said gently.

By now Carla was near to tears. Paul had been

through so much himself, and now that he had finally emerged from all that, he had landed up with having to take care of her. Would their lives together ever run smoothly?

'Will it really happen?' she said.

'Trust me, Carla, please. As soon as you're out of here, we will start planning things, and you will walk out of that church as Mrs Robinson.'

The smile that spread across Carla's face was enough to bring tears to Paul's eyes. Surely to God they had been through enough suffering by now. He held her hand tightly, and his lips moved silently as he prayed for his darling Carla to recover.

A few days later, the doctors suggested that the nurses should now start to coax Carla out of bed. They lifted her into a wheelchair and took her to the bathroom. That wasn't too bad, Carla told herself; strange thing to say, but she had enjoyed being able to sit on a toilet, and the nurses had promised that in a couple of days' time they would get her into the bath. They suggested she try to walk the short distance back to her bed. With a nurse on either side of her, she took a few steps. Her legs were like jelly, but slowly and surely she persevered, and when they got back to her room there was a lovely comfortable armchair waiting for her at the side of the bed. Gently they lowered her into the chair, and one nurse knelt and placed her furry slippers on her feet.

Paul had timed his visit well. He hadn't known of

their intentions, and the look of surprise on his face as he stood in the doorway was a joy to behold.

'Well done, my darling, full marks for your first victory,' he said before leaning down to take her hand and hold it up to his lips.

Carla felt love for this man well up within her. So often had he assured her that their wedding was going to take place in the near future and that never again would they be separated. Had she believed him? Half-heartedly, yes. But there had been so many hurdles to climb and they had caused doubts. Now she was almost inclined to believe every promise he made.

It was now a full four weeks since Paul had arrived back in England. He did not know how he would have managed without the loving friendship he had received from Carla's whole family, not to mention Arthur Townsend, the man who had already made such a difference to Carla's life.

Arthur and Paul had talked every evening, both so relieved that Carla was recovering steadily. Paul had not needed very much persuasion to go along with the plan that Arthur had suggested would be ideal for the time being.

'Where else would you take her?' had been his persistent question. 'With Mr Patterson on hand to help and Mrs Patterson to tempt Carla to eat, we should be able to manage very well.'

And so it had been settled.

Professional help had been called in, and two rooms

on the ground floor of Arthur's large house had been renovated with Carla's needs to the forefront. With all the arrangements in place, Paul went to see Dr Bannister. This doctor had been a treasure. Nothing had been too much trouble for him and his team, who had cared for Carla twenty-four hours a day since she had been admitted to this wonderful hospital.

Seated opposite Paul, Dr Bannister started to speak. 'If my team do decide that Miss Schofield is fit to be discharged, she will need to be under rigid supervision. On no account may she do anything strenuous. Complete healing can only be achieved by taking things slowly.'

He stood up and came around the desk, holding out his hand. Paul took it, lost for words. Carla had become a great favourite amongst the hospital staff. She had suffered so badly, and it had been so undeserved, but rarely had she complained.

Relief and thankfulness were uppermost in the minds of both men.

Chapter 28

Passers-by could have been forgiven for thinking that the patient leaving that day was a member of the royal family. Carla had been admired and even loved by the staff and doctors throughout the hospital. Despite the pain, she never moaned, and for the most menial of jobs that the nurses had to do for her, she'd always been ready with a thank-you. Now so many wanted to say goodbye and to wish her well.

Arthur could not have done more for Carla if she had been his own flesh and blood. In the very large room on the ground floor of his house he had gone to great lengths to make sure that every comfort possible had been provided. Some of his grandparents' Victorian furniture had been given new life, and one double bed and a single one had been installed. On either side of the huge fireplace there now stood a comfortable armchair with a padded leg rest.

Newly decorated and furnished, this room was a credit to Arthur. Massive glass doors opened on to a terrace on which stood two cane armchairs and a table. The view across the grounds was spectacular.

'Arthur has thought of everything, hasn't he?' Carla murmured.

'Yes, he most certainly has. I shall for ever be in his debt,' Paul softly answered.

Carla's first evening home could not have gone better.

Dinner had been served in their new quarters, but Arthur had taken his leave as soon as they reached the coffee stage. Carla felt deliriously happy eating with these two special men. How fortunate she was to have them both, not to mention her uncles and aunts.

Every day throughout her stay in hospital at least one of her uncles had popped in to see her. As for Edna, Daisy, Mary and Brenda, every afternoon when she had woken up from a doze there had always been one or another of them sitting beside her bed. The small gifts that had been hand-made for her and the little packets of sweets sent in by her young cousins had tugged at her heart-strings. She felt no amount of money could buy the loving companionship that existed amongst this family of hers.

And now what more could I wish for? she asked herself as she sat by the fire, opposite Paul, looking into the flames. She had wanted to sit on his lap, or at least in the same chair, but he said it was early days. What he really meant was that he was afraid he might give in to the urge to hold her tightly in his arms. That wasn't possible yet. She was still so weak and fragile.

By eight o'clock Carla's eyelids were drooping, and Paul fetched her nightclothes. As gentle as a mother with a newborn baby, he helped her to undress, and when he finally slipped the expensive nightdress that he had bought over her head, he sighed heavily. By God, he was so very grateful that she had come through this nightmare, but he was only human and he was having to keep a tight rein on his feelings. He loved her so very much, his heart ached every time he thought of the suffering she was still having to endure.

Only once during the night did Carla wake and ask for a drink of water, and Paul stayed by her side until she dozed off again.

At eight o'clock in the morning, Mrs Patterson knocked on the door to tell Paul that the nurse they had employed to visit Carla twice a day had arrived. 'And your breakfast is ready in the kitchen,' she added in a whisper.

'Thanks, Mrs Patterson, I'll be along in a few minutes,' he said before turning to face the nurse.

'I'm Paul Robinson. Carla is my fiancée. We are to be married as soon as she is better.'

The young lady in full nurse's uniform held out her hand to him.

'I'm Grace Taylor. I have read Miss Schofield's notes and I do feel for her. She has certainly suffered, but hopefully she is now on the mend. First things first, you go and have your breakfast and I will help Carla to have hers before I wash and dress her.'

Paul bent over and gently placed a kiss on Carla's forehead. 'I shall not be far away, darling, and I'll be back as soon as Grace has made you comfortable.'

When Paul returned an hour later, it was plain that Carla already trusted this nurse. He held out a small parcel wrapped up in what looked like a silk handkerchief. 'Would you undo it, please, Grace. I feel that what is inside will do a great deal for Carla's self-esteem.'

You could have heard a pin drop as the nurse gently took out a soft bright red article. She gave it a gentle shake. It was a peaked cap, but no ordinary peaked cap, that was for sure! It was made of the finest soft velvet and had a lining of pure silk.

Paul went to stand at the side of the bed. Very gently he brushed aside the straggly strands of hair that were all that was left of Carla's previous crowning glory; then, taking the cap from Grace's hands, he gently placed it on Carla's head.

Carla's hands went up, one to each side, and she softly stroked the rich material. There was a sweet smile on her lips, but her eyes were brimming with unshed tears.

'Does it feel good? Does it fit you? The peak will help to shield your eyes when the light is too bright.'

Paul only just managed to get the words out, he was so overcome with love for his Carla who had suffered so much.

'I'll clear away the breakfast tray and leave you two together for a short while,' Grace Taylor said. If the truth were to be told, she was as overcome as this young couple were.

Carla had not removed the cap from her head; her hands were still stroking it.

'Paul, darling, whatever made you think of such a thing? It feels absolutely wonderful and I bet it looks so much better than all my ragged hair.'

'Wait a moment and I shall pass you a mirror so that you can see for yourself.'

'Oh Paul, it's great. How on earth did you come to think of it, and where did you buy it? I have never before seen anything like it. Oh, it's so lovely and soft,' she declared.

'I didn't buy it. In fact, I don't think there is a shop in the country that has anything like it in stock.'

Carla was looking confused. 'So where did it come from? Somebody must care for me a great deal to . . .' She didn't get any further.

The bedroom door was now wide open, and Peggy was standing there, her arms stretched wide, her eyes brimming with tears. Paul kissed Carla's forehead and moved to leave the room, stopping only to hug Peggy as he passed.

Peggy was speechless as she gazed at her dear friend. Having taken her shoes off, she gently eased herself up on to the bed until she was sitting beside Carla. Their heads were resting on the same pillow. How long they remained like that they didn't know, and neither of them cared.

Eventually it was Carla who broke the silence. 'I really am sorry that I have not been in contact with you, Peggy.'

'No need for words like that, not between us two,' Peggy quickly assured her. 'I did come up to the hospital a couple of times, but they told me that only close relatives were allowed to see you. I didn't like to go to your family although they have always made me feel welcome. I thought they had enough on their plate without me adding to it.'

Carla squeezed her hand. 'I did wonder once or twice why you didn't come, but up until recently I was drugged up to the eyeballs and every day was the same.'

'Stop it. We have both been in each other's thoughts.'

'Peggy, have you been at home with your family?'

'No, not for ages, but by golly I did find it hard living in our workshop on my own.'

'Oh Peggy dear, it must have been so awful for you.'

'Nowhere near as bad as what you went through. I blamed myself a lot of the time. If I hadn't asked you to let me go on holiday . . . But anyway, I've settled down all right now and I have so much to tell you. I will give you a quick outline and then I am going to have to leave you, because both Paul and Arthur have threatened me that if I tire you out, they won't let me see you again. Do you remember Eddie Owen? The van driver for Harrods?'

'Yes, he is one of the nicest men. I always used to ask him in and make him a cup of coffee.'

'Oh I am so glad that you remember him, because he has been very concerned for you. He has been calling in quite regularly to see if I am coping and he has often spent an evening with me.'

'I am so pleased to hear that, Peggy. It can be very lonely on your own.'

Peggy once again felt guilty because she had left Carla, and she quickly changed the subject. 'Do you remember those samples we sent out?'

'Yes, I do. Was the comeback favourable?'

'More than we ever expected. They all heard about what had happened to you, and they have each written, not only to send good wishes but to compliment you on the samples and to offer you the chance to put on a dress show when you are fully recovered.'

By now Carla was feeling very tired, but she was pleased that their efforts had paid off and she did her best to smile.

There was a tap on the door and Paul came into the room.

'Peggy, Arthur would like you to join him for lunch,' he said quietly, seeing that Carla was fast asleep.

Peggy put her shoes on and went to find Arthur. Paul stood staring down at his beloved Carla. She was still wearing the lovely silky red cap, and it brought a smile to his face when the thought hit him that his bride-to-be looked like a little elf.

Chapter 29

Paul and Carla had been living in Arthur's house for several weeks now. Slowly but surely was still the only way forward. Paul was only grateful that since his father had died some time ago, he had become a man of means. The stock markets held his attention, and with his father's previous good experience to follow he could expect to remain a wealthy man. Although Arthur was older than Paul, a great friendship had sprung up between the two men.

The whole of Carla's family had felt relieved when the police came to tell them that the body of the man who had attacked her had been found floating in the docks. It was thought that he had been drinking heavily and had probably toppled over and hit his head before plunging into the water. Good riddance, was the general comment amongst the local people. No one on this earth was going to shed a tear for that man, let alone give him a decent burial.

Carla had tried once again to apologise to Paul that all his future plans had been set on hold because of her. For a moment he had been lost for words, and then he had knelt in front of her and tried to explain. 'Carla, how many more times must I tell you? You are my life. Without you there would be no future. As you have brought it up today, I have a suggestion, and I am going to ask Arthur to come in here and listen to what I have to say. Is that all right with you?'

Carla just nodded.

'Right,' Paul began, once Arthur was sitting with them. 'Our wedding first. It is entirely up to you, Carla. You have two choices. We could be married within two or three days if I apply for a special licence, or we can wait until you are fit and well and go for the whole big affair. Before you answer, though, there is the question of where we are going to live. We cannot continue to impose on Arthur for very much longer but I am fully aware that you wouldn't want to move too far away from your family.'

All that was met by complete silence. It was Arthur who spoke first.

'I cannot see either of you trekking around estate agencies trying to find the perfect property, and so

I am going to put forward a suggestion which you may go along with or just tell me is not for you. Either way, it will be up to the pair of you.'

This speech was met with a smile from both of them. Arthur continued.

'You are aware that in the grounds of this house there is a property that my grandfather had built for his head gardener. It was never a grand house, but it was well built and has stood the test of time, including the air raids.'

He turned to face Paul. 'I would like to give the pair of you that property as a wedding present, though you would have to keep in mind that it will need money spent on it to bring it up to meet your needs.'

Paul went to speak, but Arthur held up his hand. 'I haven't finished yet. Hear me out and then I shall listen to you.'

'Sorry,' Paul muttered, but Carla actually laughed, and that gladdened the hearts of the two men who had come to love her so dearly.

'Now to finish my proposal.' Arthur grinned. 'There isn't much land that goes with the house, and I am sure you will want to build an extension, so I am willing to sell you the adjoining acre. There, that's something for the pair of you to give thought to. I'll leave you now, no hurry for your answer.'

'Please don't leave us yet,' Carla said. Her voice held a hint of tears, but they were happy tears.

'Neither of you has said a word,' Arthur said, a glimmer of amusement on his face.

'We don't have to.' Surprisingly, it was Carla who answered. 'Oh Arthur, you have just offered me everything I could possibly wish for. To live near my own family, in a place that holds such happy memories for me. The place where you and I first met. Where every member of my family has been made welcome. You do mean it, don't you?'

'I do indeed, every word, but my dear there is one thing you have forgotten: you haven't asked Paul for his opinion.'

'Oh Paul, I am so sorry, I just naturally thought that you would jump at Arthur's generous suggestion. Please, please say that you think it is a wonderful idea.'

'Darling, I am so glad just to see you happy. As to my feelings . . . well, I cannot think of any words that could express my gratitude for Arthur's generosity.'

Turning to Arthur, he held out his hand. 'Thanks, Arthur, I shall be in your debt for the whole of my life. Just looking at Carla's face, never mind the fact that you have just offered to set us up for life . . . Well, it still seems unbelievable.'

Arthur grasped his hand. 'It works both ways, you know. The day I discovered Carla sitting outside on the steps, well, that opened up a new way of life for me. This girl could not mean more to me if she was my own daughter.' He paused and let out a hearty laugh before adding, 'And if that means that I am saddled with you because she loves you, then so be it.'

Once again the two men shook hands, and then suddenly Arthur and Paul were patting each other on the back and that led to them hugging each other. The sight of so much happiness was doing Carla a whole lot of good. Yes, her eyes were brimming with tears, but again they were tears of joy.

Carla was woken the next morning by Grace Taylor, the nurse who over the past few weeks had become a friend.

'Wake up, sleepyhead, you have two early visitors, one who is waiting to bring you in a nice cup of tea. I am going to leave you in peace for a little while. It won't hurt for you to have your bath a little later this morning.'

The door was not allowed to close behind Nurse Taylor; it was in fact pushed open much wider as a smiling Joseph made his way into Carla's bedroom.

Carla returned his smile and murmured, 'Hallo, young Joseph, how on earth did you get here?'

'Mum brought me, and she's bringing you a cup of tea.'

With that, Brenda appeared carrying a tray, which she put down on top of the chest of drawers before coming to stand by the side of the bed.

'It's a lovely day out there,' she said. 'Arthur's dusted Grandad's old wheelchair off for you, so we can have a stroll around the garden.'

Once Carla was dressed, Paul helped her into the wheelchair and tucked a blanket around her knees.

Then he and Arthur manoeuvred the chair outside, where Joseph proudly took charge, wheeling Carla carefully around the grounds with Brenda beside him chattering away and giving her niece all the family's news.

It was a memorable day for all of them. Joseph helped Arthur and Paul with various jobs around the garden, while Brenda and Carla gossiped and enjoyed each other's company. Carla felt more normal than she had done in weeks, and sitting in Grandad's wheelchair brought back bittersweet memories of the lovely old gentleman.

And later, as Paul helped Carla to get ready for bed, she felt they were even closer. Although that caused her to feel worried again. Because of all her problems, she and Paul had been acting as if they were just good friends, and she knew that was not fair on him. But she was still at a loss to know what to do about it. Later that night her face dropped as she tried to say sorry to him, but he quickly gathered her into his arms.

'My darling, dearest Carla, I am just as happy as you are, and just think about what Arthur has promised us. Our future is looking wonderful.'

Arthur had come back from seeing Brenda and Joseph off and now entered the room bringing a hot nightcap for each of them. Once more Paul and Carla tried to thank him.

'Hang on, the pair of you, there will be plenty of work to be done before you think about settling into your new home. But I want you to remember that you are not in any way disturbing me or putting me out, so if you can put up with your bed-sitting room while all the work on your new home is carried out, I am happy to have both of you under my roof.'

'Honestly, Arthur, neither of us can find the words to express what we really feel,' Carla said in a whisper. Then, changing the subject, she added, 'Wasn't it lovely to see Brenda and Joseph?'

'It certainly was. It was a wonderful day for all of us.'

Almost a month had gone by since Arthur had made his generous offer to Carla and Paul. Today all three of them were sitting on the terrace outside their bed-sitting room. To say that they were not fascinated by the hustle and bustle that was going on around them would have been far from the truth.

Arthur and Paul had been determined that they wouldn't let the grass grow beneath their feet. No time had been wasted. Arthur had contacted his solicitors, and it had been agreed that neither Carla nor Paul would have to attend the firm's premises. Any meetings at which they needed to be present would be held in Arthur's house.

That was the first problem solved. But it was only the beginning. So many papers to be signed. First and foremost was the deed of gift, to do with passing a property from one person to another. That had been a simple matter. For Arthur to sell an acre of his land to Paul involved a whole lot more work.

An architect had been brought in to prepare designs for improvements to the inside of the house as well as an extension. First things first, Arthur had insisted. A prominent firm had been approached to check over the roof and the structure of the house as a whole. Another firm had been engaged to check on the interior, and by God, what they turned up was an eye-opener. Dry rot, damp rot, woodworm. Specialists were brought in to deal with all the problems.

The acre of land that now belonged to Paul and Carla had been measured off and a boundary set up around it.

All this paperwork was a sheer necessity, but it would have been hard to say whether it was Carla, Paul or Arthur who was the most impatient for the actual work on the house to be started.

One Saturday, the Schofield family descended en masse for a visit. Sid, Jack and Albert were over the moon that Carla and Paul would be living close by. Their approval and thanks gave Arthur a warm glow, and he thought now was as good a time as any to tell the family another bit of news.

Holding up his hand, he asked for everyone's attention. 'Your beloved Carla is not the only member of the Schofield family who will be living here as soon as all the work is finalised. I am feeling very honoured to announce that Brenda has promised to marry me. Before any one of you speaks, I want to put a question to young Joseph.'

He turned to face the boy.

'Joseph, I know your mother has been speaking to you about whether she and I should get married. As you are the man of the house and have been taking care of your mum, I have to ask you, would you give your permission? I know I can never replace your dad, and you and your mother will go on loving him for the rest of your lives. What I am asking is permission to look after you both.'

The silence in the room hung heavy. Brenda's eyes were brimming with tears.

Joseph took Arthur's hand and drew him into a corner of the room. He spoke quietly for several minutes, and Arthur listened carefully. When they turned back to face the others, they were both smiling.

Arthur cleared his throat. 'The marvellous news is that Joseph has given me permission to marry his mother, though he has made one condition.'

Everyone seemed puzzled, and even Brenda looked serious for a moment.

'He has asked that he be allowed to tell the boys at school that he is to have a new father. But he also wants it made clear to some lads that have tried bullying him that his new dad is part and parcel of the Schofield family.'

There was a silence. Then Albert said, 'Joseph, why the hell haven't you said that other lads have been having a go at you?'

He didn't wait for an answer.

'Monday afternoon we shall be outside your school and we shall quietly inform them that if they think they can have a go at a member of our family, they are very wrong. We'll make it quite clear that you upset one of our family, and you upset the bloody lot of us.'

Sid and Jack were quick to agree.

'Hang on a minute.' Arthur wanted to put his two-pennyworth in. 'I think it's better that we say nothing to the kids outside the school but we quietly follow the ringleaders home and have a word with the parents.'

Joseph was smiling now, so Arthur clapped his hands for attention and called out, 'How about some congratulations? Joseph has just given me permission not only to make his mother my wife but for me to be a stand-in for his father.'

There was a mighty uproar in the room as wine corks were popped.

True to their word, Joseph's three uncles and Arthur Townsend were standing outside the school gates when he came out. His face lit up, and after a whispered conversation, Sid and Jack took their place either side of him.

They waited until Joseph had pointed out the three main ringleaders, one of whom held two fingers up and yelled, 'He's a shitty cry-baby!'

The four men would have loved to give vent to their tempers, but they were more intelligent than that. As the boys began to run, Sid, Albert and Jack followed them. They hadn't far to go. In the street of council houses, some of the parents had been forewarned and were standing at the gates. 'Here they come!' the boys shouted. 'Look, they're going to have a go at us!'

These bullying lads did not get the response they expected.

Three men came out on to the pavement; two had their shirtsleeves rolled up, and the third was stripped to the waist.

One man made straight for Arthur. 'How are yer, mate? Ain't set eyes on yer since yer set my broken arm when we were both in the merchant navy.'

Much the same thing was happening with the other two, who, it turned out, played darts with Sid, Jack and Albert in the Selkirk pub.

A hurried conversation took place and the offending boys were ordered by their fathers to explain why they'd been picking on Joseph. They were all too scared to say a word. The bare-chested man who had been in the merchant navy grabbed his son and swiftly smacked his face.

'Only a bloody coward picks on someone smaller than himself, and now I'm gonna tell yer something. He ain't got a father to look after him. Why? 'Cos he went down with his ship during the war, he was a bloody hero. So now you get down on yer knees and tell that lad 'ow sorry you are.'

'Aw, Dad, do I 'ave to?'

'Yes you do. I never thought a son of mine would turn out to be a coward. Get down before I knock yer down.'

Almost the same performance had been taking place with the two other lads.

All the men were shaking hands when Joseph tugged at Arthur's sleeve.

'All right, son I have remembered my promise.'

He looked sternly at the three boys. 'Before we go, there is something you should know. I am going to be Joseph's father from now on. He won't ever forget who his real father was, and what he did, but I shall always be around as a stand-in. So if you pick on him again, you will have me to answer to.'

He turned to Joseph. 'Come on, son, we're going home.'

Chapter 30

Ten o'clock on a Saturday morning, and to say that the grounds surrounding The Highland House were a hive of industry would be putting it mildly. Six different firms were working there, some in the grounds and some on the property now owned by Carla and Paul. The Schofield family was there in force. For the past week, delivery lorries had been arriving almost daily, and there was never a shortage of willing hands to help unload the various building materials and machinery.

So many plans had been laid that many members of the family were having their doubts as to whether even half of them would come to fruition. But as Arthur was fond of saying, money speaks all languages.

Two marriages had been arranged, both by special

licence. First, in a quiet ceremony, Carla became Mrs Robinson. There were congratulations all round, but celebrations, by mutual agreement, had been put on hold.

As he and Carla lay together for the very first time in a double bed, Paul was thanking his Heavenly Father. He had waited so long for the pleasure of having his wife lying beside him, and he was close to tears as he murmured, 'For the whole of the time I was in America, there was never a day that I didn't long for you.'

For Carla, this was the day that she had almost given up hope of seeing. But she had come through, and she knew in spite of everything that she still had so much to be grateful for.

Arthur had made sure that there was champagne cooling in their room, and Carla watched as Paul got out of bed, poured a glass and handed it to her. She took only a small sip and then set the glass down. She was now truly married to Paul, and she loved him very much and had longed for this day, but now the expectation of what he would want was terrifying her.

'Carla, please don't be scared,' Paul whispered. Standing between two beautiful flower arrangements on the dressing table there was a three-arm glass candlestick, and he put a match to the candles before he got back into bed. The candlelight transformed the room

Paul could not take his eyes off his wife's beautiful

body. This was what he had waited for, longed for, but now he was afraid he might hurt her. Yet as her arms came around his neck and they kissed, he forgot about the beating she had taken and just how close to death she had come.

They moved closer, until she was stretched out beneath him, then, ever so gently he moved until suddenly it felt as if they had become one, and Carla was no longer afraid.

Some time later, as Carla lay in his arms, all she felt was complete amazement. There had been no similarity at all to what she had feared. Now it was a new love that they shared. They had come together and everything was wonderful.

Later, Paul got out of bed to blow the candles out. As he lay down and once more took his wife into his arms, she suddenly asked, 'Paul, if I go to sleep now, will you still be in this bed with me when I wake up in the morning?'

'Mrs Robinson, we shall wake up side by side every morning for the rest of our lives. My darling wife, it has been such a long wait, but oh, so very worth while.'

Arthur and Brenda were married six weeks later, again by special licence. All four rooms on the first floor of The Highland House had been thoroughly redecorated and turned into a spacious apartment which included a large bedroom for Joseph.

Work on Carla and Paul's house had now been given priority. Meanwhile Carla's health had improved by leaps and bounds, though she was still fearful of being left on her own and never wanted Paul to be far from her sight. Nor did she like the fact that her hair was taking such a long time to grow back to its former glory, despite the efforts of her favourite hairdresser.

Paul took her on various shopping trips and sometimes had firms come to the house to give demonstrations of the goods they were selling. Carla had a wonderful time choosing furniture for their new home. She spent hours making curtains and cushion covers, rediscovering her love for sewing.

Come the day when the house was truly ready for their occupation, Paul picked Carla up and carried her over the threshold, much to the amusement of Arthur and Brenda and the various men who were still working at The Highland House.

As time went by, Paul took up a job that he had been head-hunted for. It was with a firm that had a great reputation in the financial world, a firm that his father had had close contact with. Carla fully appreciated that he needed to be occupied, but that didn't make it any easier for her to fill her own time. Mid-morning on one of the days when he had gone into the City, however, she had a wonderful surprise.

She had been watching a small car moving around the grounds, and it was obvious that it did not know where it was going. It stopped again and Carla saw a workman go and speak to the driver. The car then turned around and was now coming towards her. Carla had the front door open by the time it pulled to a stop, and her eyes almost popped out of her head. Sitting in the passenger seat was a smiling Peggy.

'Oh how wonderful!' exclaimed Carla as she watched her best friend get out and run round to throw her arms around her.

The hugging and exchange of kisses between the two young women went on for a few moments, until the driver got out and tapped Carla on the shoulder.

'Remember me?'

He was immaculately dressed in a dark grey suit, a white shirt and a deep red silk tie, and in the breast pocket of his jacket was a white handkerchief.

'Eddie Owen!' Carla exclaimed, so pleased to see him.

'Thank God for that,' he laughed, and added, 'Before we go any further, may I introduce you to my wife.'

Carla was almost speechless. 'You two got married! Oh, I am absolutely delighted. I can hardly believe it!'

The next hour was sheer pandemonium, both girls talking at the same time and laughing and crying by turns. Eddie decided to take matters into his own hands. He found the kitchen, took a percolator and a jar of coffee from the shelf and milk from the fridge, and went ahead and made three cups of coffee. Carla showed her surprise when he brought the tray into the sitting room, but Peggy laughed. 'Got my Eddie well trained,' she declared.

While they drank their coffee, the conversation turned to the subject of their workshop. There were so many questions Carla was dying to ask. Paul was of the opinion that she should never set foot in the place again, but that viewpoint did not sit well with Carla. She had put so much hard work and dedication into the business in order to get it up and running. She could not bear to think that it might all have been for nothing.

She hesitated a moment before asking, 'Peggy, have you been there recently?'

'No, not lately, but soon after you were so badly hurt, Arthur did take me there two or three times. He was very good, actually. Made sure that our sewing machines were well oiled and covered up. He also packed away all the bales of material in airtight cupboards. I think he has always been of the opinion that you would set up business again one day.'

'I wish I could,' Carla said in a soft voice that was filled with longing.

Behind Carla's back Eddie was trying to signal to his wife to leave that matter alone. However, Carla wanted to know more. She drained her coffee cup, put it down on the tray, then looked directly at Peggy.

'When you came to the hospital, you told me that all three of the upmarket stores that we sent samples to had replied very favourably. I recall you saying that they had all offered to put on a full show of our garments once I was well enough. Have I got that right?'

'Yes, dead right. They said that they liked the fact that our specimens were stylish and individual items. One firm even went as far as to say that other samples received were shoddy in comparison with our outfits. I did answer all their letters but I couldn't take up any of their offers; it was you that owned the business, not me.'

'Oh Peggy, I am so sorry.'

'For what? You weren't responsible for that man attacking you.'

'Did Arthur say anything to you about the future of the business?' Carla asked.

'Not much, though somehow I got the feeling that Paul had let him know that he didn't want you to carry on working there.'

Carla sighed. 'I know Paul has my best interests at heart, but I cannot sit here day after day doing nothing. You must know what I mean, Peggy. Anyway, let's leave that matter for now. Make sure that you two give me your new address. I am going to have a quiet word with Arthur – I respect his views. Then I shall have a good think about it before I talk to Paul.'

Peggy was looking serious. 'I do hope we can take up where we left off,' she said, her voice full of longing.

'I feel exactly the same,' Carla replied. 'I wouldn't

upset Paul for the world, but I cannot become a mere housewife, with nothing to do but dusting and cleaning. It isn't as if we haven't got bales of cloth and our wonderful sewing machines sitting idle. With all the excellent reports from our first appraisal, we should be striking whilst the iron is hot. I can't let that terrible episode ruin the rest of my life.'

Eddie felt it was time for him to say a few words.

'Carla, take it easy. You know Paul will only have your welfare at heart. Just try sitting down quietly with him and letting him know how you feel. By the way, has he ever seen your work premises, or any of the work that you and Peggy have turned out?'

The two girls looked at each other in amazement, then both shook their heads.

'Well, there you are then. Talk the whole matter through with Arthur, and between the three of you I'm sure you will eventually come up with the right decision. Might be a good idea if you all visit the premises together. Show Paul what you and Peggy have achieved. Have you still got the newspaper that gave you such an excellent write-up when you did that wedding?'

'If you haven't, I certainly have,' Peggy told them.

'Eddie, you have just made my day,' Carla told him, her face now wreathed in smiles. 'I think you have given me the best advice yet. I shall talk it over with Arthur first, and then get Paul on his own. Now, this new address of yours, is it very far away? I do hope not, because I want us to keep in touch now that we are together again.'

'Twenty minutes away. We're renting a small house for the time being, and it's working out well for me. Harrods have been really great. They phone each evening and give me a list of the work for the following day. For pick-ups it has saved a great deal of driving. When it's deliveries I do have to go into Knightsbridge to pick up, but I have been granted permission to keep my van at home, and thankfully a garage comes with the house we're renting.'

Eddie passed over the piece of paper on which he had written their address and phone number, and Carla smiled as she read it before carefully placing it in her address book. Before she had a chance to sit down again, the telephone rang, and after a short conversation she came back into the lounge grinning like a Cheshire cat.

'Nothing happens within these grounds that doesn't spread like wildfire. That was Arthur on the phone,' Carla told them. 'He said that if Peggy was thinking of taking her leave without seeing him, there'd be trouble. He suggests that we pop up to the house and then he will take us all out to lunch. He has already telephoned the restaurant and booked a table for one o'clock, though Brenda can't join us as she has gone to see Daisy today.'

Eddie looked surprised.

Peggy just smiled. 'That's our Arthur, fully in charge

at all times, and woe betide anyone who does not wish to fall in with his excellent plans.'

Arthur was waiting on the top step when Eddie drew the car to a halt. Peggy was first out and she bounded up the steps like a two-year-old, straight into Arthur's outstretched arms.

Introductions were made, and Arthur congratulated Peggy and Eddie before leading them all inside and pouring drinks. Toasts were drunk, and it was a very jovial group who finally set off to have lunch together.

The menu was impressive, with at least three choices for each course. They all did credit to their meal, and conversation was restricted until the cheese board and a pot of coffee were placed on the table. Then, it was as if someone had given permission for the subject that was so near to the hearts of both Peggy and Carla to be openly discussed.

'Arthur, as always, I am seeking your advice,' Carla began. 'I am not going to ask you to take sides but to listen to what I have to say.'

'Very well, I am all ears.'

Carla told him everything that she, Peggy and Eddie had discussed that morning, and he listened in silence, nodding thoughtfully every so often. When she had finished, there was a short pause before Arthur spoke.

'I agree with Eddie that you should show Paul the premises and the work that the pair of you have accomplished. And as for Peggy keeping the newspaper report of the wedding, well I can go one better.'

From his jacket pocket he produced two slim booklets and handed one to each of the girls. Their eyes wide, they slowly turned the first few pages, gazing at them in utter silence. Then the barrage began.

'Oh these are fantastic. You clever man.'

'However did you think of doing this for us? They are simply marvellous.'

Arthur was looking very pleased with himself as he put an arm around each of them.

'I know how hard you both worked for days on end to produce that fabulous wedding, and I thought these little books could be a record of your well-deserved success. Carla, you should lose no time in showing it to Paul.'

Carla could hardly wait. Her head was full of new ideas, and she felt ready to put them into action.

Chapter 31

Back home on her own, Carla made herself a pot of tea and sat down with the book of photographs laid out in front of her. Despite what that dreadful man had done to her, she had come through it all and she now had a life that years ago she could never have dreamed of.

Paul was her mainstay, someone so special that there was never a day that she didn't thank her Heavenly Father for having sent him to her. He was her husband, the light of her life. For weeks on end he had helped nurse her, and had shown love and patience well beyond the call of duty, but now it was as if suddenly they were on opposite sides of the fence. That just couldn't be right, and this evening she was going to bring the matter out into the open.

Paul arrived home about a quarter past six. Taking his wife into his arms, he quickly covered her lips with his, a long and passionate kiss, and when they came up for air he did not release his hold on her immediately.

'Have you had an extremely good day?' Carla laughed. 'Made some good deals?'

'Marrying you, my darling, was the best deal I am ever likely to make. How long before dinner will be ready?'

'Thirty minutes or thereabouts. I have set the drinks tray out if you would like to do the honours.'

Paul reluctantly released his hold on his wife and poured a sherry for her and a whisky and soda for himself. When they were both seated, Carla said, 'I have had a grand day. Peggy turned up with a husband, would you believe? He's someone I've known for a while; he works for Harrods as a van driver. Arthur took us all out for lunch.'

'And how did the meal go? Did Arthur approve of the marriage?'

'Very much so, and he gave Peggy and myself a gift that we both really appreciate. You can have a look at it while I go and check on the vegetables.'

Carla's hands were trembling as she handed the book of photographs to Paul. Then very quietly she left the room and went into the kitchen to set about dishing up the dinner. With a long-handled fork she tested the various vegetables, then she strained the water off and tipped them into three dishes, which she placed in the oven to keep warm while she washed the saucepans. The leg of lamb she had set out on a platter, with the carving knife and fork to one side.

Looking round, she was satisfied that everything was clean and tidy. She took off her apron and went into the hall to call out to Paul that dinner was ready, and would he like to bring some of the dishes to the table.

As usual, Paul carved and they each helped themselves to vegetables. With the exception of Paul remarking that the lamb was cooked perfectly, there was no conversation as they ate their dinner. Even while they cleared the table and finished tidying the kitchen, nothing was said. By now, Carla was longing to ask what Paul had thought about the book of photographs that Arthur had gone to such pains to produce.

In the end, her patience ran out.

'Paul, aren't you going to comment on the work that Peggy and I took on? The end result has been captured there in those photographs, and we did receive a great write-up from the local press.'

'Carla, my darling, please come and sit down. I shall fetch us both a drink, and then I shall do my best to eat humble pie.'

Carla wasn't sure that she had heard right, but by golly she was hoping that she had. Just the same, she kept her face straight and her mouth closed.

With a drink in front of each of them, Paul laid

the all-important booklet wide open in the centre of the table.

'I had no idea whatsoever as to the extent that you and Peggy must have pushed yourselves. The photographs show what stunning garments you produced, and I regret not appreciating them enough before.'

Carla was up and out of her chair and in seconds she was kneeling in front of Paul, her head tipped back, her eyes looking up into his. 'Are you saying that just to please me?'

'Certainly not. I am apologising for my lack of faith.'

'Just listening to your approval has done heaps for my ego.'

'However,' Paul continued, 'just because I think your work is of a very high standard does not mean that I necessarily approve of you going back to full-time employment. There is not the slightest need for you to earn a living; I am able and most willing to always be the breadwinner. You must realise by now just how much I love you, and I want it to be me that provides for your every need.'

He badly wanted Carla to see his side of the situation. It was with that in mind that he came up with his own solution.

'I have never even set eyes on the premises where you and Peggy work, nor am I aware of whether you own the buildings outright or if you have them on lease. If you agree, I think a meeting should be set up with everyone who is involved in the business.'

Carla nodded in agreement. 'In that case, we should begin with Arthur. He put the money up in the first place and has been behind us all the way. I suggest that you phone him and ask him to set up a meeting at the workshop, and he should invite anyone who has a vested interest to attend.'

Paul was thoughtful for a full minute. Eventually he smiled before saying, 'You, my darling wife, are a darn sight cleverer than you let it be known.'

'Maybe I have listened and learnt from you. I would like to emphasise that although I am proud of the success that has come from owning my own business, I would never allow it to affect our life together. You have to believe that much, Paul.' She grinned. 'In any case, may I now take it that you agree to my suggestion?'

'Yes, I am going to give in gracefully, at least for the time being.'

Carla felt she had boxed very cleverly by leaving all the arrangements for this meeting for Paul to sort out. She had given him Peggy and Eddie's number, and the next day she received a call from a very excited Peggy.

'Great work, Carla,' Peggy exclaimed.

'I know. We aren't there yet, but at least the men are going to talk about whether or not we start work again.'

And so the following Saturday morning found the three recently married couples assembled in Carla and Peggy's workshop. Neither Paul nor Brenda had set foot inside the building before, and they were both very impressed. Paul in particular was lost for words.

Carla managed to persuade Arthur to come into the kitchen and help make coffee. What she really wanted was to urge him to speak up for her.

'Please, Arthur,' she pleaded. 'Tell Paul how hard Peggy and I have worked to get this business off the ground. I have no wish for it to take over my life, but on the other hand I do not want to walk away from it now when success is there for the taking.'

The tour of inspection was now over and everyone was sitting down with a cup of coffee. Paul was feeling uncomfortable. He was used to being in charge of situations when at work, but here he was out of his depth. Doing his best to size up the situation fairly and squarely, he sat back and left it to Arthur to start the discussion.

'Right from the word go, the hard work and long hours these two girls put into this business went well beyond the call of duty. In my opinion, to let it just flop now would be a waste of all that effort and of their talents. You have only to look at the letters from various high-class retailers to realise that Peggy and Carla are both very gifted young ladies.'

For a minute, no one spoke. Paul had taken Carla's hand. Eddie had his arm around Peggy. Not to be left out, Brenda came up quietly behind Arthur and hugged him as she whispered into his ear, 'You, my darling, should have been in the diplomatic service.'

The rest of the meeting flew past. Plans were made and discarded over and over again. Everyone had their twopennyworth to add, and the various possible company names that were proposed for printing on their own letterhead had them all in fits of laughter.

They adjourned to the village restaurant, and Paul ordered champagne to accompany a slap-up meal. The toast was a tribute to Carla and Peggy, and their relentless pursuit of recognition for their hard work.

And so it began. Once more, both Peggy and Carla were beavering away cutting and sewing clothes for a rapidly increasing clientele. Women both locally and further afield had read of their flair for keeping up with the latest fashion, and their reasonable prices.

However, as grateful for this business as they were, their sights were set very much higher. And one morning as Carla was opening the post, she looked to where Peggy was already machining away as if her life depended on it and let out a shriek.

Peggy stopped her machine instantly. Her feet did not touch the floor as she covered the space between them.

'Where have you hurt yourself?' she almost shouted at Carla.

'I am not hurt at all.'

'Then why in heaven's name did you scream out

like that? I pictured you with your hand caught up in the machine.'

'Oh Peggy, I am so sorry if I frightened you, but you have to see this. It really does take some believing.'

Peggy took hold of the sheet of expensive writing paper, and scanned it. 'Oh my dear Lord! We are invited to visit Paris! I don't believe it.'

The two girls came together, their arms encircling each other, and stood perfectly still, not saying a word. Carla still didn't have as much stamina as she would have liked, but for that moment in time all her aches and pains were forgotten. She and Peggy now had a real future on offer and the fact that Paul was now supporting her wholeheartedly made it even better.

Chapter 32

Carla stepped into the lounge. She made a striking picture in her navy-blue business suit. Her hair, that gorgeous colour of a ripe chestnut, had been expertly cut to frame her face.

'I can't help it, Paul, I do feel sort of jittery. I wish you were coming with me. I shall phone you tonight and I should be able to tell you how long the fashion show is scheduled to last.'

Paul took her into his arms and looked down at her dear face. 'See this trip as a pre-Christmas treat as well as a wonderful boost for the business. So many dreams are about to become reality for you, Carla, and I am delighted for you. It is nothing more than you deserve.' He hesitated. 'Remember me at home on my own and don't overstay this visit, will you?'

'Of course I won't, and anyway, you know full well that the whole Schofield family will be there for you if you need them.' She gazed into his eyes. 'I love you, Paul, and I shall always be grateful that you chose me to be your wife.'

Carla sat up front in the car with Paul; Peggy was in the back seat with Eddie. The hustle and bustle at the airport brought it home to the two girls that for the first time in their lives they were going to board an aircraft.

Their suitcases had been checked in, and now they had to leave their men. Carla moved in close to Paul and murmured, 'I'll miss you.'

Paul grinned. 'You and Peggy will be having a fine old time, and you will only be on your own for three days. Arthur, Eddie and I will arrive in time for the exclusive showing, so there is no need for you to worry.'

Both girls enjoyed the flight and were slightly disappointed that it was so short. They were met at the airport by a very comfortable car, which took them to the hotel where they were to stay. Two uniformed porters showed them to their rooms, telling them that their luggage would be brought up shortly.

It was a large apartment into which they had been shown, with a bedroom each, the large beds covered by eiderdowns in a beautiful pale peach silk. They were amazed as they drifted through the adjoining rooms, opening the drawers of the dressing tables and looking at the view from the full-length windows.

A knock came on the door and two men brought in their luggage. Carla and Peggy carefully unpacked the sample items for the fashion show and hung them in the spacious wardrobes. Half an hour later, they descended the main staircase, popping their heads into the reception rooms on the ground floor. They both agreed that the hotel was sheer elegance.

'Ladies, lunch will be ready in half an hour. Meanwhile, if you'd like to follow me, I shall introduce you to a few of the people with whom you will be working.'

A tray bearing glasses of white wine was set in the centre of a large table. Lots of introductions were made and Carla and Peggy were relieved to hear that most of the conversations were being conducted in English.

By the time the day drew to a close, the two girls were thankful to be getting ready for bed. So much had been crammed into this one day, and they were both beginning to doubt their ability to take it all in. They murmured their goodnights and went straight to bed.

The next day brought home to them the reality of exactly why they were here in France. As the hours went by, the work was non-stop. The bevy of young girls who had been chosen to model the garments had to be seen to be believed. They were breathtaking: tall and slender with gorgeous long hair and glowing skin that showed not a single blemish. The number of times they had to parade up and down the catwalk was unbelievable. They listened to every instruction that was issued and moved their bodies into whatever position was requested by the team in charge of the operation.

After two exhausting days of preparation, everyone concerned voiced their approval and their thanks. Now the day of the show itself had dawned and they were all on edge, hoping that it would go smoothly.

Carla was notified that four of her benefactors had arrived and had been given front-row seats at the showing. She and Peggy were left wondering just who had accompanied their husbands on their trip to France.

The venue where the show was to take place had the appearance of a first-class theatre. Carla and Peggy were shown to seats in a box from where they could look down on to the stage where the models would parade.

'Look, look!' Peggy clutched at Carla's arm.

Carla leant over the edge of the box and followed Peggy's pointing finger. Seated down there in the front row were Paul and Eddie with Arthur and Brenda.

'Now that has made my day,' Carla said loudly.

A gentleman they hadn't encountered before made his way to the centre of the stage and made an announcement in French. Everybody in the audience started to clap, and the girls presumed that the show was about to begin.

The first garments to be displayed were all business outfits, shown off beautifully by the young models. They drew a great deal of attention from all corners of the room. After an hour or so came the interval, when champagne and canapés were served

The same well-dressed gentleman again took the centre of the stage and made quite a lengthy speech. Again it was wholly in French.

Now it was time for the evening wear to be put on show.

Two young models took to the floor together, to gasps of admiration from the audience. One of them wore a sophisticated floor-length black dress. The long-sleeved top layer was made of chiffon over a sheath of pure silk. The second dress was also pure silk, silver-grey in colour. Again floor-length, but this time sleeveless. The model carried a gorgeous little jacket which she now proceeded to put on. Its neckline and cuffs were adorned with white fur.

Carla and Peggy had made the two evening outfits, but they both gasped when they saw them modelled like this, so proud that these stunning dresses were their own work.

For the rest of the day the girls walked about in a trance, basking in the praise that came from all quarters.

Paul, Eddie, Arthur and Brenda had returned to London immediately after the show. Now Carla and Peggy were getting ready to leave too.

So many people had wanted to meet them. Everyone, speaking in English, congratulated them, assuring them that their part in the event had been an enormous success.

'Your garments will be sought after by fashionable women everywhere,' they were told over and over again.

It was a very tired but extremely happy Carla who stepped down on to English soil again and straight into the arms of her husband.

Eddie was also there, to meet Peggy. The two girls held each other tightly as they said their goodbyes, promising to meet up again in two days' time. Eddie and Paul were full of congratulations, and were certainly not backward in telling their wives how proud they were of them.

Paul had thought of everything. He had laid out Carla's nightdress and dressing gown. A bottle of champagne was waiting in an ice bucket, and two meals had been delivered earlier from their favourite restaurant, ready to be heated up in the oven.

Later, as he carried his wife into their bedroom, Paul sent up a prayer of thanks that she was safely back home. And he thanked the good Lord that her visit to France had been such a triumph.

Epilogue

Carla and Peggy had been back from Paris for seven weeks now, and they were both pleased and excited with the ongoing results of their visit. Carla was frequently telephoned by potential buyers, which meant that their garment business had every chance of growing into an enormously prosperous organisation. And the promises and predictions of the French colleagues they had worked alongside were coming to fruition. The samples that had been on show at the presentation had already attracted numerous enquiries not only in France, London and the north of England but in wider international circles as well.

In England they were approached by a number of firms to produce more everyday items. They were not tempted. That would need larger premises and a lot of employees. Carla and Peggy had talked about this, but they were as one. Both women were thoroughly satisfied with their lives. They each had a fulfilling, happy marriage. Money in the bank gave them a good, safe feeling, but they were more thrilled with the publicity and praise they were receiving for their work than with prospects of expansion. Nothing would tempt them to venture into mass-production. Their garments might be expensive, but they were guaranteed exclusive.

Carla had broken a promise she had made to herself that never again would she accept a business trip if it meant that Paul was unable to accompany her. Yet here she was up in Newcastle without him.

It was a trip she couldn't avoid: quite a large order had gone astray, and as the customer had been very reasonable and understanding, Carla felt it was up to her to sort it out personally. She had arrived yesterday and would be going home tomorrow, but first she had to get through the day.

'God knows what's the matter with me,' she said out loud. 'I just don't feel at all well.'

She put a cool hand to her forehead; it was sweaty, and now she felt sick and dizzy. 'Oh my God,' she muttered. 'When was my last period?' Suddenly she didn't want to believe what her body was telling her.

She made her way to the toilet, went into one of the cubicles and locked the door. Having pulled down her panties, she placed her hands on her bare flesh. Her stomach was as flat as a pancake. Of course it was. All the same, she knew she was pregnant. She also knew the exact moment it had happened. It was the night she had come home from France, a night she would never forget, when Paul had made exquisite love to her.

He would be over the moon, she knew. But how did she herself feel about it?

She thought about her business. She had done what she had set out to do, made a thorough success of everything she had touched. Now was a good time to start a family, for her and Paul to have a baby.

Boy or girl? What did it matter? Just to hold their child, and to watch Paul do the same . . . She folded her arms across her chest and hugged herself.

She couldn't wait to get back home. To see Paul's face when she told him the news. This was something all the money in the world couldn't buy! And it could not have come at a better time, either: just eight weeks, and it would be their first Christmas together. It had been marvellous spending that short time in France, but for the baby clothes she was going to make sure that Paul took her shopping in London. Every city in the world had different things to offer, but London . . . There had always been something special about the city that held St Paul's Cathedral and Westminster Abbey.

It was wonderful that Christmas was so close. Even

when the whole family had been short of money, the festive season had never passed without the exchange of presents, and this year it would be extra-special. She would be able to shop to her heart's content. The perfect layette, a very special shawl, a beautiful cot and of course the smartest of perambulators.

Carla was still standing there with her arms tight around her body, hugging herself. She could telephone Paul right now and give him the good news, but it wouldn't be the same. She needed to see the look on his handsome face when she told him that they were starting a family.

This was certainly going to be a Christmas to remember. And the future looked set to be filled with joy.